Call Me Ruth

"I'm glad you have a nice teacher, Rifka,"
said my mother.

"She is the best one I ever had," I told her,
"and the most beautiful."

"Maybe some day I can meet her."

I looked sideways at my mother, at her old
winter coat and hat with its faded ribbons. My
mother's shoes were scuffed and cracked
across the toes. What would Teacher think of
my mother, I wondered, but I knew the answer
even before I asked the question.

Call Me Ruth

MARILYN SACHS

SCHOLASTIC INC.
New York Toronto London Auckland Sydney

ISBN 0-590-64934-5

12 11 10 9 8 7 6 5 4 3 2 1   5 6 7 8 9/9 0/0

Printed in the U.S.A.   40

First Scholastic printing, October 1995

For
NELLIE STICKLE,
who bridged two worlds,
two centuries (I think),
and got sick
on the Third Avenue El

Call Me Ruth

Chapter 1

In the old country, my name was Rifka and my mother's name was Faigel. But when we came to America, I became Ruth and my mother became Fanny.

Our names changed at the same time but I became an American first. Even before our ship sailed into New York Harbor and I saw the Statue of Liberty holding up her lamp for me, even before that, while I was waiting for Papa to send us our steamship tickets, I was ready.

I think I was ready all the years of my life, which were eight, when the letter finally came. Mama and I were down by the river with the other women, washing out the clothes. Mama was standing barelegged in the water, her skirts hiked up around her waist, rinsing off the large, white Passover tablecloth, for the holiday had just ended.

I was standing there too, a few feet away from her, ready to help her wring out the cloth and put it into the basket on the shore.

That was when Leah, the wigmaker, came running down to the river, yelling, "Faigel, Faigel, there's a letter. Hurry!"

My mother dropped the tablecloth dripping wet into the basket and scampered barefoot back into the town. I went flying after her, but in those days my mother could run faster than I. She was already standing inside our house, holding the letter, when I arrived.

"What does it say, Mama? What does it say?"

Bubba and Zader, my grandmother and grandfather, were back there too. "Read it, Faigel," said Zader. "What does it say?"

But she stood there, holding it, looking at it and smiling. My mother smiled a lot in those days, in between laughing and crying, for she laughed and cried a great deal. For eight years, since before I was born, my father had been in America, and whenever my mother thought about him, and how long he'd been away from her, and how he'd never seen me, she cried. But when she played with me, and told me how big and strong he was, and how happy we all were going to be once we were re-united in America, she laughed.

Now she stood holding the letter, smiling at it. Her cheeks were rosy from running and her head scarf had slipped a little farther back on her forehead, showing more of her dark, curly hair than was proper for a married woman in public.

"So open it already, Faigel," my bubba urged impatiently.

Mama opened the letter and read it out loud.

"My dear wife," it said, "at last the day has arrived when I can send you the tickets that will bring you and my beloved child to America and to me ..."

That was as far as she got. My bubba immediately burst into tears.

"That I should live to see the day," wailed my grandmother. "Oh, that I had never been born!"

My mother had taken the two tickets out of the letter and was studying them gravely.

"I can't bear it," continued my grandmother, "to lose my child, my only daughter, and my little grandchild who is dearer to me than anything in this world ..."

My grandmother covered her face with her apron but you could hear the loud, muffled wails very clearly.

"Mama! Mama!" said my mother, kneeling down next to my grandmother. Now there were tears in her eyes. Through the open door, some of our neighbors had entered the house and were pressing their questions. "What does the letter say, Faigel?" "How is your husband?" "Did he send you money?" "Are there tickets?"

My grandmother seized my mother around the shoulders and began hugging her and rocking her. Soon my mother was wailing as loud as my grandmother, and in a very short time, everybody was crying too, except me.

I couldn't wait to go to America. For eight years I had been ready. I knew all about America, "The Golden Land," where everybody was rich and happy and where Jews were as good as anybody else. My papa had written and said that one day he would be a rich man too, and we would live in a grand house and have a carriage with snow-white horses.

"I wish I was dead," wailed Bubba.

I felt sorry for Bubba but I knew as soon as my mother

and I arrived in America, we would immediately make arrangements to bring Bubba and Zader over. Then they could share in our joy and be Americans too. I loved Bubba and Zader very much. We had lived with them all our lives and it was hard to say who they babied more, my mother or me. Zader was a baker and Bubba ran the store. Our house always smelled of honey cakes and sponge cakes and almond cookies. My mother and I helped Bubba with the housework but often Bubba would say, "Enough! Enough! Go!" And Mama would put on her head scarf and the two of us would run out into the fields and roll in the grass or, if it was warm enough, splash around in the women's part of the river.

Nobody else's mother acted like mine. Gitteleh, the girl next door, said my mother didn't act like a grown-up and that people said it was a shame for a married woman to play like a child. But I knew Gitteleh was jealous. Her mother yelled at her and slapped her face, but my mother made flower nosegays for my hair and sang me songs.

> Under Rifka's cradle
> Stands a snow-white kid;
> The kid went off to trade
> With raisins and almonds,
> But what is the best trade?
> Rifka's bridegroom will study,
> Torah he will study,
> Holy books will he write,
> And good and pious
> Shall Rifka remain.

For my mother had decided that I would marry a rabbi and become a rebbitzin. It was a great honor to marry a rabbi and in the evenings or on the days when we weren't outside playing, my mother had begun working on my trousseau. Under her fingers splendid flowers grew as she embroidered the tablecloth and napkins I would preside over as a married woman. Her skill as a needlewoman was widespread in our town and many a prospective bride would come to her for help.

"I want to be fourteen just like you, Mama, when I get married," I told her.

"No, no, no," said my mother. "Fourteen is too young. Papa says in America girls don't get married so young. They go to school and stay with their parents until they're older."

"Well, you stayed with your parents even though you got married. Everybody says I look like you. I want to be just like you too. I want to be married when I'm fourteen, and I want a baby when I'm fifteen, and I want to live with you forever and ever."

Mama giggled and shook her head. The light from the lamp shone on her round, red cheeks. Since nobody was in the house aside from her own family she had removed her head scarf and her short, black hair curled all around her head. She bit off a piece of string from one of the napkins she was embroidering, and held it up for me to see.

"It's pretty, Mama."

"Now you have six finished. After we get to America, I'll make you another six."

"Rest your eyes, Faigel," said my grandmother. "Have a glass of tea and a few cookies. You too, Rifka."

Bubba was always feeding us. My mother was her youngest child, born eight years after my Uncle Chaim. I had two other uncles besides him, all of whom were married. My grandmother filled our glasses with tea and nodded approvingly as my mother greedily heaped a couple of teaspoons of jam into her tea, licking her sticky fingers afterward.

"Eat, Faigel."

My mother smacked her lips over the tea, and ate four of Bubba's cookies. Bubba's eyes filled with tears and my mother said softly, "Mama, I have to go. My husband wants me to come to him."

"I know, I know," said my grandmother, "but Papa and I will be so lonely."

"We'll buy you tickets, Bubba," I said. "Right away. As soon as we get to America, we'll buy you tickets and you and Zader will come."

"No, no," said my grandmother. "It will never be. But how you'll manage, the two of you, how you'll run a household, Faigel, and take care of Rifka by yourself, I don't know."

My mother ran her tongue around her lips to round up any stray crumbs. Then she pursed her lips and pouted like a child. "I can do it, Mama. After all, I'm a married woman and a mother."

Later, when we were in bed together, and Bubba and Zader were asleep and snoring in their beds, my mother told me again about the first time she had ever seen my father. It was after all the arrangements had been made by the matchmaker, and she and he and their families had come to sign the marriage contract.

"Zader had already seen him but he wouldn't tell me what he looked like," Mama whispered to me. "I knew he was a fine scholar, a melamed, but I was afraid he might be bowlegged like Malka's husband or with a pitted complexion from the pox. Zader said no, he wasn't bowlegged and no, he didn't have a pitted complexion, but he didn't tell me how tall and handsome your father was."

"Go on, Mama, tell how he opened up his eyes when he saw you. Tell it, Mama."

"Yes, Rifka. You know better than I do. When he saw me, he opened up his eyes like two big moons. He said nobody told him about me, about . . ."

"About how pretty you were, Mama," I filled in, snuggling up against her and proud that everybody thought I looked like her.

Mama giggled and hugged me tight in her warm, soft arms. "Isn't that funny?" she laughed. "Nobody told him and nobody told me . . ."

Night after night my mother and I whispered ourselves to sleep. Sometimes my mother told me about her wedding, how her hair was braided into tiny braids with a piece of sugar at the base of each to assure a sweet life. How it was cut after the ceremony as was appropriate for a married woman, who from then on had to hide her hair under a kerchief or a wig when in the sight of strangers.

"Tell me about your gown," I urged her. "Tell me, Mama, tell me."

"You know about my gown, Rifka. You know I'm saving it for you. I worked on that gown for a year. Every piece of lace I made myself. Every embroidered buttonhole and ruffle . . . And one day, you'll stand in it under the chuppah just like me with your own bridegroom."

Some nights, and those were the nights my mother cried, she told me how my father had given up studying and decided to go to America.

"It was after the big pogrom where they broke all the windows on this street and beat up your Uncle Chaim so bad he couldn't walk for days, and killed poor Mendel, the ragpicker . . ." My mother cried and I buried my head against her shoulder and cried too.

Every Jewish child in our town knew about pogroms. There wasn't anything you could do to prevent them—no prayers to say or charms to carry. They could happen anytime and nobody was safe when they did. Only a few months ago, the Cossacks had come riding through our town on a day when I was on my way home from playing with a friend. I can remember the people screaming and the Cossacks riding over them and hacking at them with their swords. One of them came after me, his drunken face flushed and the sweat dripping from his horse's neck. I ran, and my mother's screams of "Rifka! Rifka!" guided me to her. We both hid underneath our bed, trembling at the tearing, breaking sounds and the shrieks of our friends and neighbors from outside.

"Sha, sha," my mother said, rocking me in her arms. "In America, there are no pogroms. People don't kill the Jews. Everybody is the same. Everybody is happy. That's why your papa went. He gave up studying and went away to America so we would be safe."

"Why didn't you go with him, Mama?"

"Because I was pregnant with you, and it was too dangerous."

"But after I was born, Mama, why couldn't we go then?"

"Because Papa had to find a job and get settled, and save up some money for our tickets. You don't remember your grandmother and grandfather on your father's side. They were very old and very sick and Papa was their only son. First he had to help them, and then he could save up money for us."

"And we're really going now, Mama?"

"We're really going, Rifka."

I fell asleep that night in my mother's arms, dreaming about America.

Chapter 2

"Take care of your mama," said my bubba to me just before we boarded the train. It was the end of July then. I was nearly nine and my mother was twenty-four.

After the train pulled out of the station and Mama had dried her eyes, we sat together on the bench whispering and giggling, marveling at the sights outside our window, at the unfamiliar countryside, and at the wonder of the two of us embarking on such a great adventure. Neither of us had ever been on a train before.

Soon we found ourselves famished and opened the huge bag of food that Bubba had sent along with us. Inside were roast chickens, kugel, herring, eggs, challah, jam, peaches, and great slabs of honey cake.

"It will last all the way to America," said my mother, laughing.

But the food did not last and neither did my mother's laughter. By the time we reached Hamburg, our food was gone and my mother had grown frightened and confused. We had crossed the border illegally from Russia to Germany as had most other immigrants on their way to America. Papa had written to tell us how we would have to pay a peasant to sneak us across, but he had not warned us how terrified we would be as we carried our heavy suitcases through the dark night, wondering if the border guards would catch us and shoot us. There were terrors all along the way—new trains to board, hard-faced officials to confront, more bribes, threats, and people shouting orders at us in loud, impatient voices.

It took a couple of weeks for us to arrive in Hamburg, as long as it would take for us to travel from there to America. Our food was gone, we were exhausted and dirty, but for me it was still an adventure.

"Once we're on board the ship," I told my mother, "it will be better. And soon we'll be with Papa in America."

But it was worse on the ship. Mama and I had a lower berth in the steerage compartment, and for the first week, Mama just lay there, moaning. She wasn't the only one. Our compartment reeked of vomit. So did the small, filthy washroom.

But Bubba had charged me to "Take care of your mama." So I brought her cups of water which she could barely keep down, and told her over and over again that soon her seasickness would pass and we would be in America.

I did not tell her how hungry I was. The food on board

the ship was not kosher and inedible in any case. If it wasn't for Golda, one of our fellow passengers, I might have starved to death by the time we reached America. Golda was a small, thin woman who slept in the upper berth with her two little children. She took pity on me and shared her bread and onions and herring with me. I tried to help her with the children in between looking after Mama.

"That's very beautiful," Golda said to me one day, admiring a red and blue embroidered shirt I was wearing.

"My mother made it for me," I told her.

She sighed. "I'm not handy," she said. "Other women have golden hands, like your mother. But me, I can't even sew a straight seam."

"My mother is famous in our town for her needle-work," I boasted. "Nobody makes such beautiful embroidery designs. Sometimes brides used to come and ask my mother to sew for them. She's making me things for my trousseau."

"I would like to see them," said Golda.

I showed them to her. I opened one of our suitcases and spread out the wonderful tablecloth that my mother had made just for me with the blue, silver, and white border of scrolls and flowers, and the six finished napkins. "She's going to make me six more napkins when we come to America."

Golda shook her head with admiration over the table-cloth and napkins and held them carefully in her hands as if they were made of gold.

Sometimes Golda sat with my mother while I took her two children upstairs on the deck of the boat. There, everything smelled better although you could usually find somebody hanging over the railing.

The days were warm and the nights calm. Everybody said how lucky we were that the weather held and there were no storms. Sometimes, at night, when the compartment grew stifling hot and foul with the smell of unwashed bodies, I brought my blanket upstairs and slept out on the deck under the stars. They shone as big and bright as the stars in my old home in Russia. In America, I knew, they would shine even brighter.

Suddenly, after a week, my mother woke up one morning feeling better. She washed herself quickly in the cold, salt water provided in the washroom, changed her clothes, and came upstairs with me on the deck.

"Ah! Ah!" she said, gulping in the clean ocean air. "Ah!"

She ate some of Golda's bread and drank some tea and smiled. Up and down we walked together on the deck and my mother's pale cheeks began to grow rosy again. At night, with other passengers also sitting out, my mother began singing some of the old songs from Europe. Her voice was strong and beautiful. Soon others joined in. Somebody got up and danced and I did too while my mother sang:

> *Dance, dance opposite me*
> *And I will dance with you;*
> *You will take the son-in-law*
> *And I the daughter-in-law.*

My mother always knew more songs than anybody else and that night she sang first one song, then another. It was the happiest time I had spent since leaving home. And other nights followed. Down inside the boat, the air was stifling. The old and sick lay helplessly in their hard berths. Hungry children cried and the stench of dirt was overpowering.

But upstairs, the warm days and mild nights continued. We stayed on the deck most of the time now, and my mother was petted and admired for her pretty face and happy songs. I danced every night and fell asleep cuddled up against my mother's warm, soft side, hearing her singing.

The final day came, still warm and bright with sunshine. People laughed and joked but some of the passengers worried.

"Ellis Island," they said. "That's where they stop you. That's where they send you back. If you have lice in your hair or if you don't stand up straight—for nothing at all, they send you back."

My mother and I tried to wash all the parts we could reach on that morning. The basins in the washroom were crusted over with dirt and I shut my eyes while I washed so I wouldn't have to look. But I wasn't afraid like the others. They would never send me back. Not me and not my mother. We were both healthy and strong. And we had my papa waiting for us. Waiting to take us to our new home in America.

New York City. That was where we were going to live. A big city—the biggest city in America, maybe in the world. On our way across Russia and Germany we had seen other cities with big buildings and many, many people hurrying back and forth. But New York City would be the biggest and the best. I practiced saying it, "Noo Yawk Ceety." And I practiced other English words that I whispered to myself as I dressed in the only remaining clean clothes that we had left for this day. "Goot day, Papa" and "My name iss Rifka" and "How doo you doo?"

Mama had a picture of Papa which she carried in her suitcase. A big, handsome man with a black beard and a thick head of dark hair Mama put on her sheytl, the wig that married women wore to cover their hair, smoothed down the creases in her long-sleeved blue dress, and pulled her flowered blue shawl around her shoulders.

"You look nice, Mama," I told her.

She patted my hair and tugged at my jacket. Then she looked me over carefully as I stood stiffly, awaiting her approval. She smiled. "Your papa will be so proud," she said.

"Will he be there on Ellis Island?" I asked her.

"No, no. But after . . . if everything goes all right . . ." Her face wrinkled with worry lines.

"It will be fine, Mama. What could happen?"

"They say if they find anything wrong with you . . . if you have a rash or something wrong with your eyes . . . they say for nothing at all they can send you back."

"Don't worry, Mama, we'll be fine," I comforted her.

On Ellis Island, they put signs on us and herded us into metal pens. The officials shouted at us, "Quick!" "Hurry!" "Move there!" They pushed and prodded us as if we were sheep. A few times we were nearly separated and my mother shrieked, "Rifka! Rifka!" and clung to my arm.

Doctors stood there as we moved along in narrow rows. They held colored chalks in their hands and if anyone limped, or coughed, or looked suspicious, they marked him with a big colored letter and pulled him out of the line.

"Where are you going?" an official asked my mother in Yiddish. She hesitated and he said sharply, "Speak up!"

"To . . . to . . . join my husband."

"Where does he live?"

"In New York City."

He motioned her on impatiently. Then he turned to me. "What is your name?"

"Rifka."

"How old are you?"

"I'm eight now but in a few weeks I'll be . . ."

"Move along! Move along!"

Other doctors poked at us with stethoscopes, pulled at our hair, and, worst of all, tugged hard at our eyelids, twisting them back over a hard stick and peering into our eyes. My mother gasped from the pain during her eye examination, and there were tears in my eyes when they had finished with me.

"Move along! Move along!"

"Hurry up! Quick! Quick!"

More questions. "Any crazy people in the family?" "Any criminals?" "Any anarchists?"

But we were coming to the end of the line. A few more pokes and prods, another few questions, and we would leave Ellis Island behind us.

"Good-bye! Good-bye!" I began calling to some of the friends we had made on board the boat. Golda, our good, kind friend Golda, was going to join her husband in Buffalo. Who knew if we would ever see her again? On ship that morning, she and my mother had cried over each other and wished each other nachas. But back there, on the line, they had pulled out one of her children and put a colored chalk mark on him. Something was wrong, and in our last sight of Golda, she was holding onto one of the doctor's arms, crying and pleading while he tried to shake her off.

"Move along there! Hurry!"

But now we were being herded onto the ferry that would take us to New York City. To Papa. To America.

We stood on the front of the ferry, carrying our bags and suitcases. Mama stood up very stiff and straight as we watched the New York skyline grow closer and closer and closer. There were people waiting at the dock. First you could see only the shapes of heads and then as we drew closer the heads developed eyes and noses and mouths.

"Is that Papa, Mama? Is that him?"

"Where? No, that's not Papa."

"There, Mama, there, waving his hat."

"No, your papa is taller and younger and more handsome."

We carried our baggage off the ferry. Around us people hugged and kissed and laughed and cried. It was hard to move in all that crush of people and baggage. But we pushed on, looking around us.

"Do you see him, Mama?"

"No, not yet. But he knows we're coming. He'll be here." Her cheeks were deep pink.

"Is that him, Mama, coming toward us?"

"No, Rifka, that's not him. Hold onto me tight, but also, don't lose your suitcase."

My heart was beating high up in my throat. Any minute now my papa whom I had never seen, my own papa would come and find us. He would enfold us in his big arms and kiss us and I would say to him . . .

"Faigel!" someone was calling.

My mother spun around and screamed, "Shmuel!"

A man was pushing his way through the crowd. He was not a tall, powerful man with a dark beard and black hair. Not a big, handsome man but a slight, thin one with a pale face and graying hair.

"Shmuel?" said my mother.

But the man was grabbing her, kissing her, and crying, "Oh, Faigel! Such a long, long time! Oh, Faigel!" And then he was kneeling by me and hugging me and kissing me and holding me away to look at me and pulling me close again to kiss me. His face was wet from his tears and he said, "My little Rifka, my little daughter!" So I knew it was my father even though he didn't look at all like the picture in my mother's suitcase. And I said to him in English, "Goot day, Papa. How doo you doo?"

Chapter 3

My mother cried for days and days. She said it was because somebody had stolen the beautiful tablecloth and five of the napkins meant for my trousseau. Mama thought it had to be Golda.

"And to think," she wept, "that I thought she was an angel, sharing her food with us, looking after me when I was sick . . . Such a wicked woman!"

"But maybe it wasn't Golda," I said. "Maybe it was somebody else."

"No, no, no," my mother cried. "It was Golda. All the time she wanted to look at my sewing. All the time she only wanted to hold it in her hands."

"You'll make another one, Faigel," said my papa.

"For two years, I worked on that tablecloth. I made up

the design myself. Nobody ever had such a beautiful cloth."

"You still have one of the napkins, Mama," I comforted her. "You can work out the pattern again from that."

"And Rifka is not even nine years old yet," said my papa. "You'll have plenty of time to make her another one. Besides, in America people usually buy their wedding things in a store."

My mother shook her head and continued weeping. Even in America, she said, there was no store that would have a tablecloth and napkins as beautiful as the stolen ones. So she cried and said it was because of the theft, but I knew that she wept for other reasons as well.

In Russia, we lived with Zader and Bubba in a small house. We all slept in the same bedroom and the store was part of the house. But everything smelled of sweet cakes and outside lay the green fields and the trees. Here in New York, the place that my papa brought us to was an apartment up four flights of stairs in a dirty, dark building. Only one of the rooms had windows. The other two smelled of mold. Everything was gray in the apartment, and even the windows looked out on wash lines that crisscrossed over a dark alley without sunshine.

"I was very lucky to find this place," said my papa. "Look at this furniture. I bought it for next to nothing. The woman needed the money. Her husband had deserted her, just walked out on her, and left her with four children. So she had to sell everything. She was desperate. I paid only twenty-five dollars, and just look!"

Proudly, Papa showed us the chairs and tables, the beds and dishes, the curtains hanging at the windows. Pictures of people we didn't know hung on the wall.

"Everything," said my papa, "she sold me everything. Even the pictures. We can use the frames. One day we'll put our own pictures in—of you and me and Rifka."

My father was so happy. All the time Mama was crying, he was laughing. He kept kissing her and me. He kept pulling me into his lap, and telling me how he had longed for me, how he had dreamed of holding me in his arms. He showed me a baby picture Mama had sent him and he told me how he looked at it every day. "But now you're here," he said, "and one day soon, the three of us will take a picture together."

I loved my father right from the start. Even though he didn't look anything like the picture Mama carried with her, he was even better than I had dreamed. He loved America just the way I did, and he loved being an American. Right away, he wanted Mama and me to be Americans too.

He taught me some new words in English. "Thank you" and "Please" and "Pardon me." And he gave me my new name in America.

"Ruth," said my papa. "From now on your name is Ruth, and Faigel, your name is Fanny."

Mama cried when Papa told her about her new name. She cried when he told her that American women did not cover their hair with a wig or a scarf. That they wore hats with feathers instead.

"We have to keep up with the times," said my father, "which is why I shaved off my beard. It seems strange at first, Faigel—I mean, Fanny—but you'll get used to it and you'll be happy. You'll learn the new ways and we'll save our money and soon I'll go into business for myself and we'll move uptown or out to the country in Brooklyn."

My papa was full of plans to make us all rich and happy and after a while, my mother stopped crying and started listening. Papa showed her how to use the coal stove in the kitchen and how to keep food in a funny box called an icebox. She listened to him tell her about all the wonderful new foods people ate in America, and she tried to taste a strange, slippery fruit called a banana.

"Feh!" she said, spitting it out of her mouth.

My papa laughed, and to please him, I ate a piece and swallowed it.

"My little Ruthie," said my papa proudly. "She's going to be a real American."

That night for the first time in my life, I slept apart from my mother in the small room beyond the kitchen. It seemed strange to be sleeping away from her but I was so tired that I dropped off to sleep immediately. In the middle of the night, I woke up because somebody was sitting on my bed, and tears were falling on my face. It was my mother.

"What is it, Mama?" I said, sitting up. "Is something wrong with Papa?"

"No, no, nothing is wrong," sobbed my mother. "Everything is fine. Go back to sleep."

"So why are you crying if everything is fine?"

"I don't know," said my mother.

"Aren't you happy to be here in America, Mama? Aren't you happy to be with Papa again?"

"Yes, I am," my mother cried. "Only he's not well. He's sick. He coughs. He looks like an old man."

"But that's because he missed us so much," I said. "Now that we're here, he'll feel happier and he'll look better. We'll take good care of him."

But my mother kept on crying.

"Shh!" I said. "You'll wake up Papa."

So she crept into bed with me and whispered, "I miss Zader and Bubba."

"But we'll bring them over too," I whispered back. "We'll save money like Papa said, and we'll bring them over."

"I don't like it here," my mother said. "It doesn't smell good here in America."

"We'll get used to it, Mama. You'll see. And soon, like Papa said, we'll move out to the country."

After a while, she stopped crying and I drifted off to sleep again. When I woke up in the morning she had gone back to the big bed in the bedroom.

All the next day, friends and relatives came to visit and welcome us to America. They brought cookies and cake and fruit. Papa's sister, Tanta Sadie, whom I had never seen, and her husband, Uncle Barney, came early in the morning with their children, Joey, Morton, and Shirley. I knew Shirley was just my age, and I was impatient to meet her. But when she came into the apartment, dressed like a real American girl in a plaid ruffly dress and with a big red bow in her hair, I felt shy and leaned against my father and listened while they spoke to each other at first in English.

"The important thing," Tanta Sadie said, finally speaking in Yiddish to my mother and me, "is not to look like greenhorns."

Her eyes rested on my mother's wig when she said it, and then traveled over our Old World dresses and shawls. "Right away," she said, "you have to buy some new clothes, Fanny, for you and Ruthie here. School is going to start next week and she can't go looking like a greenie."

My mother nodded helplessly. "Tomorrow," said Tanta

Sadie, "I'll come and take you out. We'll go shopping and I'll show you where all the good stores are."

My Uncle Barney reached into his pocket and gave each of his children a penny. Then he gave me a penny too. I studied the copper-colored coin in my hand and the strange-looking face on it.

"That's Pocahontas," said my cousin Shirley to me in Yiddish. It was the first time she had spoken to me directly. I didn't know who Pocahontas was and I certainly couldn't repeat the name. But I didn't want to appear stupid so I nodded and smiled. Shirley went on. "Pocahontas was a beautiful Indian girl who saved the life of Captain John Smith." I still didn't understand but I kept on nodding and smiling.

"Do you want to know what it says on it?" Shirley asked. "I can read it for you."

She pointed with her finger to the words above Pocahontas' head. "That says 'United States of America' and over there is the date. See, it's a new coin from this year, 1907. Now come downstairs with me and I'll show you how to spend it."

I stayed close to Shirley as we walked through the busy, crowded streets. I had never seen so many people jammed together in my whole life. There were pushcarts and stands lining the streets, filled with books, clothes, fruits, vegetables, and pieces of fabrics . . . "Five for a nickel," "A penny a piece," "Come and buy," "No place cheaper." Everybody was yelling and nobody seemed to be listening.

Shirley led me to a candy stand on one corner where rows upon rows of strange, marvelous candies lay. I had never tasted any of them before but my mouth began watering.

"What do you like?" Shirley asked.

"Everything," I told her.

She helped me make a selection. "Those little butterscotch squares are eight for a penny, and those chocolate mints are four for a penny, and those pieces of licorice are six for a penny, and those gumdrops are also six for a penny. Why don't you get two butterscotch squares, one chocolate mint, and three gumdrops for your penny. I'll get three pieces of licorice, two pieces of halvah, and one peppermint stick for mine, and we can share."

Later, we sat on the stoop of my house, eating our candy and Shirley told me about school.

"I'm going to be in Miss Bartlett's class. She's supposed to be very nice. Last term, I had Miss Anderson and she was mean. Once, she rapped my knuckles just because I passed a note to my friend Charlotte Goodman."

I thought about my school back in the old country. Girls didn't need to go to school for very long—only a couple of hours every day for a few years. They taught us how to read and write Yiddish and only enough Hebrew to read the prayers but not understand what we were reading. Only the boys were really educated. In the old country, girls grew up to be wives and mothers.

"My brothers go to a different school—for boys," said Shirley, "but everybody learns the same in America. It doesn't matter whether you're a girl or a boy." She made a face. "I don't like school but Mama wants me to go to high school."

"What's high school?"

"It's where you go after grammar school. If you go to high school, you can work in an office when you graduate, or you can go to college if you want to be a teacher."

"Even if you're Jewish?" I asked. "And even if you're a girl?"

"Everybody is the same here," said Shirley. She tossed her long curls and her ribbon bounced on the top of her head. "I want to be an actress when I grow up and have a pink dress with a train made out of lace and a matching pink parasol and a pink hat trimmed with white ostrich feathers."

I ate my candy and listened as my cousin Shirley described all the clothes she was going to buy when she became rich and famous. Maybe I would grow up to be rich and famous too, but in the meantime, I kept looking at my cousin Shirley's red and green plaid dress and wondering if my papa would buy me a dress just like that.

The next day my Tanta Sadie and Shirley arrived to take us shopping. Tanta Sadie wore a determined look on her face as she announced to Mama that she must not wear her wig ever again.

"Throw it away," she said. "Burn it."

"But Leah, the wigmaker, made it for me," my mother protested. "She used the best hair in the village."

"Do you want everybody to know you're a greenie?" asked my aunt. My mother remained silent.

"We'll buy you a nice hat but for now, in all this heat and around the neighborhood, you don't have to wear anything on your head."

My mother shuddered, wrapped a scarf around her head, and pretended not to notice my aunt rolling her eyes up to the ceiling. Tanta Sadie was a tall, stout woman with a large mole on one side of her nose. That day, she wore a stiff, white shirtwaist and a black skirt and she crackled when she walked.

"Shirtwaists are all the style now," she informed my mother. "Ever since the turn of the century, every woman has at least several shirtwaists and skirts in her wardrobe.

There are some women, high-class women too, who only wear shirtwaists and skirts. I think we will begin by buying you a couple. And you should let your hair grow now that you won't be wearing a wig." She reached up and patted the bun at the back of her head. "American women like to grow their hair long."

Shirley was wearing the same green and red plaid dress she had worn the day before. I said to my aunt, "Tanta Sadie, I would like a dress just like Shirley's." My aunt nodded approvingly at me. "We'll go over to that store. It's only a few blocks away. He has a very nice selection of clothes for girls, even though he's a ganuff. You have to let him know right away that you know he's a thief and you want the best price or you'll go some other place. Just leave it to me. We'll get Ruthie a few dresses and some pinafores and then she'll need shoes and stockings and underwear . . ."

"But the money . . ." my mother began.

Tanta Sadie held up her hand. "You've got a good husband, Fanny," she said. "He's saved and borrowed and gone without all these years just for you. Yesterday he put some money in my hands so we could go out and buy you American clothes. He doesn't want to feel ashamed when he introduces you to his friends and neighbors."

Mama argued over each item of clothing Tanta Sadie said she needed, but I didn't argue. I certainly wasn't going to let my dear papa feel ashamed of me. We ended up buying three dresses for me—two plaids and one pale blue for going out. We also bought two white pinafores, some long black stockings, a pair of high-buttoned shoes, and petticoats and underwear. One of my dresses was the red and green plaid just like Shirley's.

That night, before my father came home from work, Mama and I dressed up in our new clothes to surprise him. Mama folded up her good blue dress and shawl from Europe and my embroidered blouses. She patted them and stroked them as if they were good friends, but she wrapped them in paper and put them away in the wardrobe in the bedroom. She wrapped up her wig in newspaper and put that in the wardrobe too. She shook her head and sighed, but she did it.

"So many buttons," moaned my mother as she and I worked on each other's clothes and shoes. But finally we stood together on our tiptoes, trying to get a glimpse of ourselves in the small mirror over the chest in the bedroom. We could only see ourselves from the hips up but Mama said the lower parts of me looked fine and I said they looked fine on her too.

Papa came home at eight. We could hear his quick steps running up the stairs. His face was flushed and his eyes shining as he burst through the door.

"My boss let me off early tonight. He had a lot of work but he knows this is the first day you were left alone and . . ." He stopped and stared at us. Mama was blushing like a young girl and smiling a shaky, little smile. She stood there, her head down, peering out at him, unsure of herself and at how he would find her in the new American clothes. She wore a white shirtwaist buttoned up high on her neck and a sleek, black skirt that showed off her small waist and round hips.

"Oh, Fanny, my beautiful Fanny," Papa murmured and kissed her.

"Look at me, Papa. Look at me," I shouted, tugging at his arm.

"Like a real American girl," he said proudly.

It was a happy night. Mama hadn't prepared anything for supper, but we ate bread and herring and some of the cakes and cookies people had brought over the night before. Later, we took a walk through the warm, steamy night, wearing our new clothes, and Papa stopped from time to time to introduce us proudly to our new neighbors. "This is my wife, Fanny, and my daughter, Ruth. This is my family."

Chapter 4

By Thanksgiving, I had written a poem and had become Teacher's pet. The poem went like this.

THANKSGIVING
by Ruth Zelitsky

To be an American I am proud
And happy that I can say it aloud;
In Europe I was only a slave
But now I live in the home of the brave.

I am thankful that now I am free
There's nothing in America I can't be;
Hooray for the red, the white, and the blue,
To this country I will always be true.

My teacher, Miss O'Brien, had me read it out loud to my own class. Then she sent me down the hall to read it out loud to Miss Stewart's regular 4B class.

When I had finished, Miss Stewart smiled and nodded at me. Then she turned and looked with disgust at the students sitting in her own classroom.

"I wonder," she said to them, "why it is that nobody in this class has ever written a poem?"

She waited but no answer was forthcoming.

"Here we have a nine-year-old girl who has been in this country less than three months," said Miss Stewart, "and is still in one of the special classes for new Americans. Yet she is able to write a fine poem. I think you should all be ashamed of yourselves."

Later, in the hall, some of Miss Stewart's students told me very clearly what they thought of my poem and me. But I was not discouraged.

I loved school. I loved my class with the beautiful letters written on charts around the room and the sound of the chalk squeaking on the blackboard when Teacher wrote out our spelling lessons. I loved when it was my turn to stand up and read out loud and to watch Miss O'Brien's special smile of approval. In Europe, a girl was important only as a future wife and mother but here in America a girl, and especially a smart girl, could be just as important as a boy.

I hungered for school. On weekends, I couldn't wait for Monday to come. Right from the start, on that first day when nothing Teacher said made sense, even then, I loved school. Our simple readers with their bright pictures of dogs and cats and apples were entrancing. "See the dog run." "See the red apple." "The snow is white." I turned each page and studied each new picture and each new word with enchantment.

And every morning when we saluted the flag and recited the Pledge of Allegiance, my voice was the loudest.

I pledge allegiance to my flag and to the Republic for which it stands, one Nation indivisible, with liberty and justice for all.

One day I was a little, ignorant, immigrant girl who sat in my class at school and understood nothing, and the next day, it seemed, I had become a real American and could understand everything.

But speaking English was not as easy as understanding it.

"De snow is vite," I read out loud.

"The snow is white," corrected Miss O'Brien, sticking out her tongue for the *th* sound and shaping her lips into a round circle for the *w*. "Now I want to hear everybody in the class repeat with Ruth, 'The snow is white.' "

"De snow is vite," chanted my classmates and myself.

"The," said Miss O'Brien wearily.

"De," repeated the class.

"The!"

"De."

Miss O'Brien said that good Americans brushed their teeth twice a day with a toothbrush, that they bathed frequently, shined their shoes, cleaned their fingernails, and never wore dirty underwear. "Cleanliness is next to godliness," Miss O'Brien told us and so did the nurse when she came to examine our hair for lice.

"I never knew from toothbrushes in Russia," I told Miss O'Brien when I stopped by her desk one afternoon. Often I liked to linger after the other children had gone.

"I never knew *about* toothbrushes," she corrected.

"And now I shine my shoes every Monday," I bragged, "and I clean my nails. And every Friday, I go with my mother to the Educational Alliance for a shower."

"Only once a week?" asked Miss O'Brien. "Can't you go more often?"

I blinked when Teacher said that because I thought a once-a-week shower was almost excessive.

"You have no bathtub at home, do you, dear?" Miss O'Brien asked gently.

"No, Miss O'Brien. We have a sink in the kitchen with water but it's too small to take a bath in. Our toilet is in the backyard. I wish we had one in the hall like in my cousin Shirley's house. Every floor has its own toilet in her house."

Miss O'Brien frowned and began shuffling her papers. I could see she didn't like talking about toilets. I wondered if maybe good Americans weren't supposed to talk about toilets. So I asked her.

"Is it a bad thing to talk from toilets, Teacher?"

"*About* toilets, dear, and yes, it isn't very polite in this country."

"I won't do it anymore then, Teacher."

Miss O'Brien patted my arm comfortingly. "You are making amazing progress, Ruth. I don't think I've ever had a student as quick and willing as you. I think you'll be ready to go into the regular class in a few weeks."

The week before Thanksgiving, Teacher taught us a serious song.

> *We gather together*
> *To ask the Lord's blessing;*
> *He chastens and hastens*
> *His will to make known . . .*

And one to sing for fun.

> *Over the river and through the wood,*
> *To Grandfather's house we go;*
> *The horse knows the way*
> *To carry the sleigh*
> *Through the white and drifted snow . . .*

We drew pictures of turkeys and horns of plenty, and Teacher told us how she was going to spend the holiday with her parents and brothers and sisters. Her parents lived in the country, and every Thanksgiving all the children and grandchildren gathered at their house for the Thanksgiving feast. She described the menu to us— roast turkey with stuffing, cranberry sauce, mashed potatoes, home-baked rolls, salad, and apple and pumpkin pies. She told us how the dining room table would look, covered with a lovely, clean white cloth, the family china, and sparkling glasses.

"Ever since the Pilgrims came, Americans have always held a feast and thanked God that He brought them here to America," Miss O'Brien said.

I told my father and mother about Thanksgiving and what Miss O'Brien had said. "All Americans are supposed to have a feast and be thankful," I said.

My father said he would be working on Thanksgiving, and my mother said nothing.

"Mama," I asked, "why couldn't we prepare a feast and celebrate when Papa comes home from work?" I described to her the different kinds of food Miss O'Brien and her family would be eating on Thanksgiving.

My mother looked up at me from her sewing. There was a large pile of men's jackets on the kitchen table and she was finishing the buttonholes and collars. More and more now, during the busy season, my father brought home clothes from work to finish at home. He still had not paid off all the debts he had incurred from bringing us over and setting up our own household.

Papa was a tailor and worked on men's suits. Every morning when there was work, he left the house at seven-fifteen to walk to his shop by eight o'clock. Some nights he came home at eight and sometimes even later. Whenever he brought work home, he might stay up until midnight finishing it. Mama worked with him. During the day too, he left a pile of clothes for her to finish and often when I came home from school she would be sitting there, sewing by the kitchen table. She never had any time to work on my trousseau. It worried her. The stolen tablecloth and five napkins were very much on her mind but as Papa often told her, "There will be plenty of time when we pay off our debts."

"I don't know," said my mother, helplessly, "what it means—Thanksgiving."

"Mama," I said impatiently, "I told you already. It's a holiday when Americans say thanks to God because He brought them over here to America."

"I don't know," my mother repeated, shaking her head.

"You have to go to school, Fanny," said my father. "I keep telling you. Go over to one of the classes at the Educational Alliance. Take off an hour a day. Learn to speak. I did when I first came. I went for a couple of years and now I can speak as good as anybody and I know all about the American holidays."

"I'll go, I'll go," my mother promised and she bent her head over her sewing again.

My father and I looked at each other, and then he said,

"Maybe Sadie is going to make a Thanksgiving dinner. Maybe she'll ask us."

"No," I told him, "Shirley said they're going to Uncle Barney's cousin's house. Papa, why can't we have our own Thanksgiving dinner? I'll help Mama. Please, Papa!"

"Well!" My papa looked doubtfully over at my mother. He didn't say anything but we both knew that my mother was not a balabusta, not a woman who was either a good cook or an accomplished housekeeper. Bubba had been right. My mother tried but managing a household was still difficult for her.

"Please, Papa! Teacher says all Americans are supposed to have a Thanksgiving dinner."

"So what do you say, Fanny?" asked my papa. "It will make Ruthie happy."

"But I don't even know what it is," my mother cried. "Cranberry sauce and pumpkin pie? I don't know."

"I'll help you, Mama," I said. "I'll go shopping with you. We don't need the cranberry sauce and the pumpkin pie. And we don't have to make the rolls either. Please, Mama!"

My mother did not exactly say yes but my father and I began making plans. "Maybe," said my father, "I can go in at six in the morning and get off a little earlier at night. And maybe I can ask Sol Becker to come too. He works next to me in my shop. Poor man, he's all alone here and he has no family. Like I was all those years. But now—I've got my family. I really have something to be thankful about."

I sat in my father's lap while my mother kept sewing and the two of us worked out the details for Thanksgiving. I would come right home from school on the Wednesday before Thanksgiving and go shopping with

Mama. Papa said we should buy a chicken instead of a turkey since it would cost less and besides we were only going to be four people. On Thursday, Mama and I would do the cooking, fix up the house, and set the table. Papa said he would buy a cake and some rolls in a bakery on the way home from work and maybe even a bottle of schnapps.

Mama and I went to the chicken market on Wednesday afternoon. We inspected the live chickens in their crates, all clacking away at the tops of their lungs. Mama couldn't make up her mind. "I don't know," she kept saying, "I don't know." Finally, I picked one out—a noisy one with angry little eyes.

After the butcher had slaughtered it, I helped Mama pluck it. She began laughing as the feathers tickled our noses and made both of us sneeze. It felt good to be laughing again with my mother. We walked back through the crowded streets that day before Thanksgiving, rubbing up against other shoppers. We stood in front of pushcarts and bought our potatoes and our carrots and we argued about the prices and my mother's cheeks turned rosy again and her eyes shone.

On Thursday, I helped Mama clean the house. All the scattered papers and clothes I shoved under my parents' bed or stacked in a corner of their bedroom. Mama sang some of the old Yiddish songs from Europe as she worked.

> *I've fallen in love with a handsome lad*
> *Who shines like the midday sun,*
> *Oh, Mother dear, it's him that I love,*
> *He's the only possible one.*

"You should learn some English songs now that you're an American," I told my mother.

"I will, I will," she promised.

"I'll teach you one for Thanksgiving," I told her and began singing "Over the River and Through the Wood."

"Ofer de river and true de vood," my mother repeated.

"No, no, no," I corrected, just like Miss O'Brien, and showed her how to hold her lips to form the *th* and the *w*. My mother always learned new songs quickly and soon the two of us were singing it together.

When we set the kitchen table for dinner, Mama spread out a tablecloth that she had embroidered for her own trousseau before she was married. It was a very beautiful one with a center design of red and gold flowers. But my mother shook her head sadly when she looked at it. "The one I made for you," she said, "nobody ever saw a tablecloth like that."

I brought out the one napkin that remained and spread it open on the table. Both of us bent over it and studied it. There were blue and white flowers connected by a delicate silver stem with silver leaves. My mother's fingers stroked the flowers lovingly. "At least," she said, "that wicked woman left me this one so I can remember the pattern. It's a good thing it got separated from the others and was hidden under the stockings. Otherwise she would have stolen it too. For that, at least, I should be thankful."

"See, Mama," I told her. "We all have something to be thankful for. That's why today is Thanksgiving."

As we set our table, I thought about the Thanksgiving table in Teacher's house, about the fine white china, the sparkling glasses, and the heavy silver. On our table, only Mama's tablecloth was beautiful and festive. Our dishes were cracked and unmatched and the glasses were dull and of different sizes. But I knew in the years to come, when my papa became rich, we could buy a set of dishes and some shining glasses. Then our table would look just like Teacher's. I could wait.

By seven o'clock, all was ready. The potatoes and carrots simmered on the stove and the chicken baked and baked inside the oven. Mama and I dressed in our good clothes and waited for Papa in the warm, fragrant kitchen.

He came at seven-thirty with his friend Sol Becker.

"Mmm!'' he said as he came through the door. "Something smells wonderful." He smiled as he looked around the tidy kitchen, at the table set for dinner, and at Mama and me, all dressed up in our good clothes. Proudly, he introduced us to his friend.

The men washed up at the sink.

"Sit! Sit!" Mama ordered the two of them. She bustled around as if she was an experienced housewife.

"A schnapps, Sol?" asked my father. "You'll have a schnapps with me? After all, it's Thanksgiving."

Sol's long face drooped and he sighed.

"Don't worry, Sol," my father said. "Your turn will come too. All those years I waited for my loved ones and now here they are. It's like a dream come true. The same will be for you. You'll work hard and save your money and in another year or so, you'll have your wife and children with you too."

Mama brought two little schnapps glasses and Papa filled them to the brim. He held his up and so did Sol Becker. "L'chaim!" they both said. "To life!"

Sol Becker cheered up a little after another schnapps. My papa said how lucky they both were to have jobs when so many were unemployed.

"But our boss is a momsa," said Sol Becker "He pays us starvation wages and squeezes every drop of blood out of us."

"But we're working," insisted my father, "and one day our turn will come too."

"Maybe so, but in the meantime I'm going to join the union."

"Don't be a fool," said my father. "If he found out you joined, he'd fire you. He'll never allow a union in his shop."

"If enough people joined," said Sol Becker, "we could make him. It's not right that he pays us for ten hours of work and keeps us twelve hours or even fourteen sometimes. It's not right for him to keep piling on more and more work and telling us to work faster and faster. And the shop is so dirty you can hardly breathe. In the summer you could choke from the heat and in the winter you could die from the cold."

"Well, well," said my father. "He's a hard man but he started out the same way we did, and look at him now."

"God forbid I should ever be like him. God forbid I should ever forget what it feels like to slave over a sewing machine all day long and make barely enough to make ends meet."

But my papa was looking with pleasure at Mama and me as we carried the food to the table. There was plenty of it even if the chicken was burned, the stuffing tasted like straw, and the mashed potatoes were dry and lumpy. It didn't matter that my mother still had not mastered the stove. Today was a special day—our first Thanksgiving in America.

Chapter 5

My papa's cough grew worse and worse as the winter progressed. Some mornings he coughed so much he could barely drag himself out of bed. The doctor came, listened to my father's chest, and shook his head.

"So, Doctor?" asked my father. "What should I do?"

"What should you do?" said the doctor. "You should take your yacht, sail to the Riviera, and spend the winter there, lying on the beaches and eating caviar."

My father smiled and said, "Not yet, Doctor. Maybe in a few years, but in the meantime?"

"In the meantime," said the doctor, "I told you before. You have 'The Tailor's Disease.'" The best thing for you would be to go to the sanatorium in Colorado. I know a doctor there. I could write a letter for you."

"And my family? Who will take care of my family?" asked my father.

"That's what I thought you would say," said the doctor. "So here's a prescription for cough medicine. Take it three times a day. Try to stay warm and get plenty of rest."

That winter, my father bought another sewing machine for my mother. He taught her how to sew on it and she learned quickly. His own sewing machine he carried back and forth to work whenever he had a job. My mother now sewed at home during the day and often at night, finishing clothes he brought home for her. Often the kitchen and the other rooms were strewn with pieces of thread and material. They mingled with the dust that settled more and more heavily on the windowsills, the tops of the furniture, and even on our pillows in bed. But some weeks my mother made as much as three dollars and my father was pleased.

In school, I had been promoted into a regular 4B class. Miss Lyons, my new teacher, smiled a great deal more often than Miss O'Brien, gave us all little pink candy hearts for St. Valentine's Day, and let me wash the blackboards. So everybody knew I was teacher's pet.

We learned long division, fractions, and decimals and I got 100% on all my test papers. I brought them home and showed them to my parents, and I also showed them the compositions I wrote with Teacher's comments of "Excellent" or "Outstanding." Sometimes my father took my papers into work to show the men at his shop. He was the first one I told about my new plans for the future.

"Papa, I think I want to be a teacher when I grow up."

"Why not?" said my father. "With your head you can be anything you like. And in a few years, when I have my own shop, maybe we can even buy a piano and you can take music lessons."

We started learning about history in fourth grade. Teacher told us stories about famous Americans like George Washington, Abraham Lincoln, and our President, Theodore Roosevelt. We read about them too in our book *Great Americans for Little Americans*.

I liked to share my stories with my parents, usually at night when the three of us sat together in the kitchen near the stove. Papa and Mama sewed while I did my homework to the chattering sound of the sewing machines. Every so often, they would stop and listen to me.

"Did you know, Papa, that George Washington never told a lie?"

"I think I heard that before."

"Teacher told us today that when he was a little boy he wanted some cherries that grew on a cherry tree in his father's orchard. So he chopped down the tree and ate the cherries. Later, when his father came home, and he saw that somebody had chopped down the cherry tree, he was very angry and he hollered out, 'Who chopped down my cherry tree?' George Washington knew his father would beat him but because he was so honest he stepped forward and said, 'Father, I cannot tell a lie. It was I. I chopped down the cherry tree.' And you know, Papa, his father was so pleased he told the truth that he didn't beat him."

"But why," asked my mother, "did he chop down the tree in the first place?"

"I don't know why, Mama," I said impatiently. "But the important thing is he told the truth."

"I think he was stupid to chop the whole tree down just for a few cherries. He could have climbed the tree and picked them," said my mother.

"But Mama, that's not the point. Don't you see—he told the truth. That's the point."

My mother shook her head and went back to her sewing and my father and I smiled at each other over her head.

For Washington's Birthday that year, there was going to be a special assembly program. Each fourth- through eighth-grade class would select one outstanding student to stand up on the stage in the auditorium and recite a poem or speech in honor of the occasion. Miss Lyons picked me. I couldn't wait for my father to arrive home that night. Even before he was completely inside the door, I yelled out the news.

"Papa, Miss Lyons picked me to recite a poem for the Washington's Birthday Assembly Program. Only me! She picked me out of everybody in the class. She said I deserved it the most because I'm the best in the whole class. That's what she said, Papa. I'm the best."

My father had tears in his eyes when he heard the news. He shook his head back and forth with pride.

"Teacher said I should recite a poem," I told him. "She picked one out from a special book and she copied it down for me."

"I only wish I could be there," said my father, "to hear you. I would be so proud."

"And I think I'm going to be the first one on the program. Teacher thinks I would make a good impression if they started with me."

"If only I could hear you."

"You will hear me, Papa. I have to memorize the poem, and you can help me."

Over the next few nights, my father held the copy of the poem and listened attentively as I recited it.

THE SHIP OF STATE
by Henry Wadsworth Longfellow

Thou, too, sail on, O Ship of State!
Sail on, O Union, strong and great!
Humanity with all its fears,
With all its hopes of future years,
Is hanging breathless on thy fate! ...
In spite of rock and tempest's roar,
In spite of false lights on the shore,
Sail on, nor fear to breast the sea!
Our hearts, our hopes, are all with thee,
Our hearts, our hopes, our prayers, our tears,
Our faith, triumphant o'er our fears,
Are all with thee—are all with thee!

Teacher wanted me to speak with a lot of expression. It was easy for me because the words were so stirring. Every time I said "Sail on" I poured into it all my passionate love for America.

"You say it so beautifully," sighed my father, "it gives me goose pimples just listening."

I never did recite the poem for the Washington's Birthday Program. Instead, Sarah Plotkin said it and the whole class wrote me a letter saying how sorry they were to hear the tragic news.

My father had died.

On Sunday before the Friday when I was to recite the poem, my father listened to me for the last time. I knew the poem by heart and Papa said, "You can't say it any better than you did tonight. But we'll go on rehearsing it together for the rest of the week so you won't forget "

Monday it rained all day, from early in the morning

when my father left for work until eight o'clock at night when he returned home, shivering and coughing more than usual. He couldn't even eat supper but went right to bed.

"Tomorrow, Ruthie," he said in a hoarse voice, "tomorrow, we'll practice."

But Tuesday he was too sick to get up and the doctor came. He told my mother it was pneumonia and prescribed some medicine. My father couldn't even talk to me on Tuesday night when I stood there by his bed and listened to him gasping for breath.

Early Wednesday morning I woke up to the sound of my mother's screaming. My father was dead.

My mother screamed and wailed and called out his name in Yiddish. "Shmuel! Shmuel!" she cried. Not Sam, his English name, which he preferred, but Shmuel. During the day when the women came to prepare the body for burial, my mother sat huddled in a corner of the room, crying and screaming. She didn't stop as we stood in the cemetery the next day in the rain, as they lowered the coffin into the earth. And back at the house, she continued crying and screaming.

"It's enough already," said Tanta Sadie, Papa's sister, whose own eyes were red and puffy from weeping. "You'll make yourself sick."

But my mother could not be consoled. Even while we sat shivah for seven days, the prescribed period of mourning, and friends and relatives came, bringing cakes and fruits and good things to eat, telling funny stories, and trying to get her mind on other things, my mother never stopped.

"You have to pull yourself together, Fanny," Tanta

Sadie said. "For the sake of your child, you have to stop. It won't bring poor Sam back again, and you can't afford to make yourself sick."

Tanta Sadie remained with us during shivah. She did the cooking and cleaning, for my mother was incapable of doing anything. When friends and relatives came to visit with us, Tanta Sadie was the one who talked to them. My mother could not be distracted from her grief.

"Maybe if you told her to stop," my aunt said. "Maybe she'd listen to you."

My mother had pulled out her old blue-flowered shawl from Russia that she had worn ever since she was a young girl. She had worn that shawl when she first met my father and now she sat, wrapped up inside it.

"Mama," I told her, "Mama, Papa wouldn't want you to go on like this. Papa would want you to try a little harder."

But my mother just rocked back and forth inside her shawl, weeping and not answering.

At night, I slept with her in the big bed in the bedroom and my aunt slept in my old bed in the little room. The whole house had been dusted and aired, the floors washed and swept since Tanta Sadie had come to stay. All the dust and lint had been swept away but the rooms still smelled damp and moldy.

My mother cried herself to sleep every night. Nothing that I said seemed to help.

One night, about six days after my father's death, my mother woke me up. She put her arms around me and whispered, "Rifka, wake up."

"What is it, Mama?" I whispered.

"Listen, Rifka," said my mother. She always called me

Rifka even though I told her over and over again that I wanted to be called Ruth. "Listen, Rifka! Are you awake?"

"Yes, Mama, I am," I said. Even though it was the middle of the night and I was very sleepy, I was pleased to hear that my mother was speaking without weeping.

"I want to talk to you, Rifka. I want you to listen to me."

"All right, Mama. I'm listening."

"I'm going to talk low because I don't want to wake up Tanta Sadie."

"All right, Mama, I can hear you."

"Rifka," said my mother. "I want to go home."

"What do you mean, Mama?" I asked her. "You are home."

"No, no, I'm not home. Home is Russia, not America. Home is my town and my mother and father and a better life than this. This isn't home."

"No, Mama!" I said. "No!"

"Listen, Rifka. Listen, Mamala. Your father would be alive today if he hadn't left home. Maybe it's not so good there. Maybe there are pogroms and a Jew isn't exactly a human being but at least you can live there. You can breathe the air and the sky is blue. Here you can't live. It's not good here. I want to go home."

Then I began screaming. For the first time since my father died, I screamed. "No! No!" I yelled. "I won't go. I won't! I won't!"

"Sha, sha!" said my mother. "You'll wake Tanta Sadie. Listen to me! Listen!"

But I wouldn't listen. It was bad enough that my father had died and that I had not recited my poem at the Washington's Birthday Program, but now my mother, my own mother, was trying to take me away from my beloved country. "No! No!" I shrieked. "I won't go. I won't."

Tanta Sadie came flying into the bedroom. "What's wrong?" she cried. "What's wrong?"

I was kicking and thrashing around on the bed.

"Sha, sha, Rifka," my mother said.

"And don't call me Rifka," I yelled. "My name is Ruth, and I won't go. I won't."

"What's wrong?" my aunt asked, sitting down on the bed.

I leaped into her lap and buried my head against her shoulder. "*She* wants to go back to Russia. *She* wants to take me back with her. But I won't go. I won't go. Oh, Tanta Sadie, don't let her take me back with her. Let me stay with you."

I could feel my aunt's body stiffen against mine. Then, slowly, her hand began patting my back.

"I didn't know," came my mother's voice, very small, like a guilty child's. "I didn't know she would get so upset."

"What did you expect?" said Tanta Sadie, continuing to stroke my back. "I can't imagine, Fanny, what you were thinking of. To wake a child up in the middle of the night . . ."

"I'm sorry." My mother's voice was very soft and low. "Come back to bed, Rifka. We'll talk another day."

"No, no," I yelled. "I don't want to go. Never. Not now. Not another day. I'm an American. I'm not a foreigner."

"Fanny!" warned my aunt.

"All right, all right!" My mother's hand touched my shoulder but I shrugged it off and clung to my aunt.

"That's all right, Ruth," crooned my aunt. "Let's just forget the whole thing and go back to sleep now. It's three o'clock in the morning and we'll all catch cold if we keep sitting here."

My mother tried to talk to me but I put my fingers in my ears and wouldn't listen. In the morning, it was decided that as soon as we could sell our furniture and make all the necessary arrangements, my mother and I would go to live with my Tanta Sadie and her family. My mother never said anything more about returning to Russia.

Chapter 6

Tanta Sadie was a balabusta. She scrubbed the oilcloth floors every other day, washed the windows in the parlor once a week, boiled our clothes clean and ironed them stiff and scratchy with starch. Her house smelled of cleanliness and of good food cooking. When she had nothing else to do, she polished her kitchen stove until the nickel trim gleamed so bright you could see your face in it.

No dust gathered on Aunt Sadie's windowsills or the top of her furniture. Even the corners of the floor and underneath the beds were so clean you could eat off it as she frequently boasted.

Only the cockroaches and the bedbugs put up a real fight against her. Aunt Sadie scrubbed the walls with ammonia and washed the bedsprings with kerosene. In the winter, the enemy retreated but every summer, along with the hot weather, they returned.

"It's Mrs. Kaplan's fault," Tanta Sadie said bitterly, motioning with her head toward one of the rear apartments. "She's such a slob. The other day, I caught her throwing garbage down the air shaft so I hollered out to her, 'Mrs. Kaplan, if you don't stop that, I'm going to call the police.' "

"So what did she say, Mama?" Shirley asked.

"She acted surprised. Like how come I was blaming her. Like she wasn't the one who was doing it. So I told her, 'Mrs. Kaplan, maybe you don't mind living in a filthy pigsty but I won't stand for it.' "

While she talked, Tanta Sadie's fingers were busy at the kitchen table filling cheese blintzes. First she took a circle of yellow dough and dropped a heaping tablespoon of sweetened pot cheese into the center. Then her fingers rolled and folded the ends of the dough until it turned into a little plump cylinder.

"Mama," Shirley asked, "can we go to Coney Island today?"

"No, Shirley, not today. Maybe tomorrow."

"It's so hot, Mama," Shirley whined. "We didn't sleep all last night and the bedbugs kept biting us."

Tanta Sadie began mumbling again about Mrs. Kaplan but then Shirley said, "Mama, can we sleep on the roof tonight?"

"I don't think so, Shirley. It's too much trouble."

"Please, Tanta Sadie," I begged. "I didn't sleep either last night and neither did Joey. He was wheezing all night long."

"It's like an oven in those bedrooms," Tanta Sadie said.

Little drops of sweat outlined her upper lip and her forehead glistened. "Who can breathe in such heat?"

"Please, Mama," Shirley said. "We don't have to carry up our mattresses. We can sleep on an old blanket like most people do, and just take up our pillows."

"It's so filthy on the roof," said Tanta Sadie, "and you'll get tar on the pillowcases."

"No, we won't, Tanta Sadie. We'll be careful."

"Well . . ."

"Please!"

"All right, all right. We'll see. Now go away and play and don't bother me."

Shirley gathered up her jacks and we hurried outside before she could change her mind. Whenever Tanta Sadie said, "We'll see," it usually meant yes.

"Anything you ask for," Shirley said to me, "she'll say yes."

Ordinarily, none of us was ever allowed up on the roof. Only last week, down the block, a boy had fallen off and died. But in the summertime, whenever it was very hot, Shirley said, lots of people slept out on the roof.

"It's like a party," she told me. "People tell jokes and sing and dance."

"Like on the boat coming over," I told her. "Most nights we slept out."

"I don't remember the boat," Shirley said.

"Because you were only a baby when you came, but it was wonderful. The stars were so big and bright and every night we sang and danced. Especially when my mother sang. Everybody really had a good time when she sang. She knows more songs than anybody else."

"I never heard your mother sing," Shirley said

We sat down on the stoop in front of our house and

Shirley threw out the ten jacks and bounced the little red ball up in the air. Up the street, somebody had turned on the fire hydrant, and children in their bathing suits and some even in their underwear ran in and out of the gushing stream of water.

"Look!" said Shirley. "There's Marsha in her underwear."

Marsha was our age, nearly ten.

"She's too old to go around in her underwear," I said. "It's not very refined."

"She should wear a bathing suit," said Shirley. "If she wore a bathing suit it would be all right."

"On the street?" I said. "A girl her age? Maybe it's all right for little children but for a girl who's nearly ten . . ." I shook my head but Shirley continued watching.

"She's really having fun. Oh, look! Joey Pincus just pushed her head under. Look! Look!" Shirley began laughing.

"Maybe tomorrow Tanta Sadie will take us to Coney Island."

Shirley stood up. "I'm going upstairs and get into my bathing suit. Come on, Ruthie."

"No," I told her. "I think we're too old."

But Shirley ran upstairs. I sat there watching the children shrieking and splashing under the fire hydrant. Their faces glistened and their hair lay cool and plastered on their heads. My mother and I used to splash each other like that when we played in the river of our town in the old country. I remembered the delicious feel of the cold water on my hot skin and I thought maybe I should get into my bathing suit and join all the others.

"Come on, Ruthie," Shirley said when she came downstairs in her bathing suit and slippers. "Don't be so stuck-up. Don't always act like you're better than everybody else."

She hurried off and I watched her long curls bouncing on her back as she ran. The other children called out to her as she approached and Joey Pincus and another boy came out from underneath the spray to drag her screaming, but laughing, into the stream of water.

I watched as the water from the gushing hydrant exploded against the bodies of the children and ran in quick streams down the sides of the street. The water, clear as it came from the hydrant, turned black as it flowed down the filthy street, gathering up pieces of paper and garbage as it went.

Disgusting, I thought, but I longed to go and play and splash with the other children. Something always held me back and made the others call me "Stuck-up!"

I gathered up the jacks and walked back up the stairs to our apartment. Tanta Sadie was stirring a pot of beet borscht on the stove.

"Is that you, Ruthie?"

"Yes, Tanta Sadie."

"Are you going to change into your bathing suit too?"

"No. I think I'm too old to go in my bathing suit on the street."

Tanta Sadie smiled and shook her head at me. "Such a little lady you are, Ruthie. I wish Shirley was more like you."

Now I felt better. Tanta Sadie's approval was worth more than Shirley's scorn.

"I think I'll sit out on the fire escape and read," I told my aunt.

"What are you reading, Ruthie?"

"It's a book about the pioneers. I just took it out of the library yesterday."

"Be careful you don't fall."

I eased myself out on the fire escape and settled down against the railing. Four stories down, the street was pocked with people. I could see Shirley and her friends still splashing by the hydrant. Their screams and laughter floated all the way up to me.

"Hello, Ruthie," said Mrs. Berman, who was sitting out on the fire escape next to ours. She was a very young woman with a brand-new baby who lay sleeping inside of a wall of pillows.

"Hello, Mrs. Berman."

"Isn't this heat terrible?"

"I don't mind it so much. But my aunt says we might go to Coney Island tomorrow and maybe we can sleep on the roof tonight."

"I've been sleeping up on the roof all week. It's the only place you can get a breath of air. But they make so much noise, it wakes the baby."

I opened my book and began reading.

"What are you reading, Ruthie?"

"It's a book called *Stories of American Pioneers*."

"You're some reader, Ruthie!"

Everybody in the building knew I was smart. Everybody thought I was special. I settled myself comfortably on the fire escape with my legs sticking through the bars and read about the trials and hardships of our brave American pioneers. They didn't waste time splashing in front of fire hydrants while they cleared the wilderness. And their children studied hard and grew up to be great men and women—teachers, doctors, and even Presidents.

A few soap bubbles floated up from the fire escape below where my cousin Joey and his friend Morris were blowing bubbles.

"I see Ruthie's bloomers," my cousin chanted.

I wrapped the skirts of my dress carefully around my legs and ignored him. What could you expect from a boy!

Twice a week during the summer I went to the public library for books. The librarian, Miss Cooper, knew my name and even smiled at me and saved books for me. She didn't know Shirley's name and she never saved books for Shirley. If it weren't for the library, I would have been desperate. I missed school. I couldn't wait for September. The long summer days dragged on and on. Only my books kept me occupied.

Aside from my cousin Shirley, I didn't really have any other friends. But I didn't need any. Shirley had many friends. They were always knocking on the door and asking Tanta Sadie if Shirley could come out to play. Sometimes I would go along, especially if they agreed to play school. I was always the teacher when we played school.

I would lead them downstairs to the stoop and sit them down in rows on the steps. Then I would stand up very straight and stiff and speak very clearly.

"The class will now rise and salute the flag."

Or I would teach them to sing, waving my arm in time to the music.

> *Happy spring, bright and gay,*
> *Winter now has passed away,*

making sure everybody said winter and not vinter.

"You're like a real teacher," Shirley said. But lots of

times she called me stuck-up and complained that her mother liked me better than her.

We slept together in one of the beds in a small windowless bedroom. The boys slept in the other bed. Tanta Sadie and Uncle Barney had the other bedroom all to themselves and my mother slept by herself in a cot in the parlor.

"Soon," Tanta Sadie said, "we'll move uptown and find a bigger place, maybe even with a toilet in the apartment." Tanta Sadie was always making plans like my papa used to. She liked nice things but there was little money left over after she bought food for all of us. Uncle Barney was a cutter in a ladies' cloak and suit shop. He had a friend whose sister worked as a sewing machine operator in a shirtwaist factory. She found my mother a job in her place as a "learner" and now money wasn't quite so scarce and Tanta Sadie didn't grumble so much about how hard it was to make ends meet. My mother made six dollars a week as a learner, but Tanta Sadie said if she did good work and wasn't lazy, one day she could make as much as ten or even twelve dollars a week.

We didn't wait for my mother or Uncle Barney that night for supper. Tanta Sadie had chilled the borscht in the icebox. She served each of us a bowl with sliced cucumbers and a pat of sour cream floating in the center.

"I'm too hot, Ma," Joey complained. "I don't want to eat anything."

"Eat!" ordered Tanta Sadie.

After the borscht came the cheese blintzes. Joey kicked at the table and fiddled with his food. Of all of us children, Joey was the thinnest, the sickliest, and the pickiest eater. Tanta Sadie regarded him with irritation and alarm.

"You'll die if you don't eat," she warned him.

"It's too hot, Ma."

"Eat!"

The sweat was dripping down my back but I took another cheese blintz and began eating it.

"Look at Ruthie. See how good she eats. Why do you think she's so smart?"

"I hate blintzes and I hate Ruthie."

Tanta Sadie smacked Joey and he jumped up and ran off screaming from the table.

"Such a heat!" Tanta Sadie said, finishing the blintzes on Joey's plate. "A person can't even live in such heat."

When it was dark, we brought our pillows up to the roof, and spread out an old blanket to lie on. The roof was filled with our neighbors. Some of the grown-ups were smoking cigarettes, others were playing cards, and the children moved back and forth and over the walls that separated one rooftop from the other

"Be careful! Don't lean over! You'll fall! Be careful!"

Lighted cigarettes glowed bright in the darkness. But up above, the stars flickered dimly not nearly as bright as they had appeared on board ship or back in the old country.

Someone played a harmonica and somebody else an accordion. The singing began—old songs from Europe and new ones like "In the Good Old Summertime" and "Shine On, Harvest Moon."

Uncle Barney came upstairs with Tanta Sadie. They brought some more pillows and Tanta Sadie said she thought it was time we children went to sleep. But nobody could sleep.

"At least you can breathe here," said Uncle Barney, sitting down on a blanket and lighting up a cigarette.

"It must have been over a hundred degrees at work today. Two of the operators fainted."

Tanta Sadie made sympathetic noises and said maybe it would cool down tomorrow.

"I was dripping wet all day. There wasn't a dry spot on me. But the boss wouldn't let anybody go home on time. He had a big order so we had to work over."

"Maybe you should try to sit near a window," said Tanta Sadie.

"Everybody wants to sit near a window," said Uncle Barney.

Mrs. Kaplan, who threw garbage down the air shaft, and Mrs. Rosenberg from the second floor front began singing "Meet Me in St. Louis, Louis" and a few people got up to dance. Mrs. Kaplan's voice was sweet and high but not nearly as beautiful as my mother's.

"Where's my mother?" I asked Uncle Barney. "Didn't she come home yet?"

"Yes, she did," said Uncle Barney. He looked around the roof. "I don't know where she is. Did you see her, Sadie?"

"Maybe she's still downstairs," said Tanta Sadie. "I told her to eat something before she came up."

"I'll go down and see," I told them. I moved through the open roof door and down the stairs to our apartment. When I opened the door, the hot, heavy air inside nearly choked me. "Mama!" I called.

She wasn't in the kitchen and I called again, "Mama!" Nobody answered.

"Mama!"

The lamp in the parlor had been lit and my mother lay stretched out, fully dressed, on her cot. She was asleep, her hair damp and sticking to her head.

"Mama!" I called. "Mama, wake up!"

She opened her eyes and looked at me as if she didn't know who I was.

"Mama, come upstairs. It's cooler upstairs. They're singing songs and dancing. Come on, Mama. Come upstairs and sing."

My mother sat up and licked her lips. "I'm too tired," she said. "I want to sleep."

"Come on, Mama. You wash up and eat some supper and you'll feel better."

"It's too hot," said my mother.

"You'll die if you don't eat," I told her, just as Tanta Sadie had told Joey earlier that evening.

So my mother stood up, washed her face and hands at the sink, and tried to eat the borscht and the blintzes.

"It's too hot," she said, shaking her head. "It's too hot."

But she came up on the roof with me. They were still singing and dancing. I waited for my mother to join in. I even told Shirley, "Wait until my mother sings." But my mother never sang at all that night. She lay down on one of the blankets and slept. She lay in her clothes and they looked soiled and wrinkled. Her mouth fell open as she slept and she made snoring noises. I tried not to look at her.

Chapter 7

About a year after my father died, Tanta Sadie began to nag my mother about her appearance.

"What do you always want to dress like a shlump for? You're a young woman yet. Take a little pride."

My mother was puzzled. "I have enough to wear," she said. "For work, it's good enough."

"But you don't have anything for going out."

"Going out?" said my mother. "Where do I go out? Six days a week I go to work and on Sundays I stay home to do the washing and ironing and to help you a little . . ."

"You stay home too much," my Tanta Sadie said. "You're a real stick in the mud."

"And you never went to school like you promised,"

I chimed in. "You still talk Yiddish. You'll never learn English if you don't go to school."

"But Rifka," said my mother, "I get home so late from work and I'm always so tired. There's no time."

"Call me Ruth!" I told her. "And some of the classes start at eight or eight-thirty at night. You could go if you wanted."

"You don't want Ruthie to be ashamed of you," said my Tanta Sadie. "She's a real little lady. Look how she takes care of herself. I don't even have to tell her to change her underwear or wash her feet. Look how she keeps herself and look at you."

My mother looked at me and I looked at her. Of course, I couldn't see myself but I knew that everything I wore was fresh and clean. Even underneath, where you couldn't see, my petticoats and bloomers were spotless. My mother, on the other hand, had bought hardly any new clothes since we first arrived in America. She had grown careless in her grooming; her shirtwaists had faded and her skirts never looked pressed.

"You have to have a little pride," said my aunt.

One night in early spring when I was seated at one end of the kitchen table doing my homework, and my cousins were playing pisha paisha on the other end, somebody knocked on the door. It was a young woman, dressed neatly in a black coat and hat. She asked for my mother.

As usual, my mother was lying down on her cot but she stood up, came into the kitchen, and looked questioningly at her visitor.

"How do you do, Mrs. Zelitsky. My name is Leah Rubin."

"Oh," said my mother.

"Sit down, sit down, Miss Rubin," said my aunt, clearing a little space at the kitchen table, and beckoning for my mother to do the same.

"I work in the same shop as you, Mrs. Zelitsky," said Leah in Yiddish.

"Oh," said my mother.

"Would you care for a glass of tea, Miss Rubin?" said my aunt. "I know it's kind of chilly out tonight."

"No, thank you, Mrs. . . . ?"

"Mrs. Feldman. I'm Fanny's sister-in-law."

"No, thank you, Mrs. Feldman. I can only stay a little while. I have some other people to visit tonight too."

My mother sat down next to the young woman and waited.

"I can understand that you don't know me, Mrs. Zelitsky. After all there are two hundred of us who work at Ace Shirtwaist Company, and we never have much time to get acquainted."

"I tell Fanny she should make a little more of an effort to get to know some people," said my aunt. "She's a real stick in the mud. But it's very nice of you to come and visit her."

Leah smiled at my aunt but she said to my mother, "Can I ask you something, Mrs. Zelitsky?"

"Yes."

"How much of a wage do you make?"

"I make six dollars a week usually, but less in the slack season."

"How long have you been with the company?"

"Over a year now."

"You're still a learner then?"

"Yes," my mother sighed, "but I can sew as well as anybody else. I keep telling the foreman it's not fair that

I should be paid as a learner when I do even more work than a regular operator. But he just tells me to wait."

"How much do you make, Miss Rubin?" demanded my aunt.

"I can make twelve dollars when the season is good. In my last job, I worked on samples and sometimes I made fourteen, fifteen dollars a week."

"See, Fanny," said my aunt. "The same thing will happen to you. Maybe you have to work a little faster so they see how good you are."

"I worked for four years as a learner before they let me get paid as a regular operator," Leah said. "My work didn't change. They keep you as a learner as long as they can so they don't have to pay you a decent wage."

"Four years?" said my aunt. "How old are you?"

"I'm nineteen but I had to go to work when I was twelve. My father died and I was the oldest. My mother had five younger ones so we had to live on my miserable wages until my brother was twelve and he went to work too. Those were hard years, I can tell you."

"My Rifka," said my mother fiercely, "I'll never let her go to work. I'll die before she has to slave in a factory."

"Don't worry about me," I said loftily. "I'm going to finish school and be a teacher."

"That's just what I used to say," said Leah Rubin.

I decided I did not like her. I opened my book and pretended to resume my homework, but I listened as she continued talking to my mother.

"Do your eyes hurt you?" she asked.

My mother shrugged her shoulders. "The light is very bad where I work. You know there are only windows in the front of the shop and just a few of the experienced girls manage to work there."

"And your fingers?"

"Well," said my mother apologetically, "it's not so bad anymore. In the beginning when they rushed me and I had trouble keeping up, then the needle used to go through my fingers all the time. But now it only happens once in a while when I'm tired at the end of the day. It's not so bad. I'm used to it. The worst part is when the needle breaks and the boss makes me pay for it."

My mother's hands were lying on the table. They were large, coarse hands with broken fingernails. Some of the fingers were blistered and covered with scabs. They didn't look anything like my teachers' hands.

Tanta Sadie said, "It's hard on her. She never had to work like that in the old country. But what can we do? She's a widow with a child and my own husband barely makes enough to support us. What can we do? I hope one day she'll find a good man and . . ."

"And they'll both suffer together," said Leah Rubin.

"So what is it you want, miss?" asked Tanta Sadie.

"I want you to join the union, Mrs. Zelitsky."

"Union!" Tanta Sadie laughed. "Union! My husband belongs to the union and a lot of good it does him."

"Mrs. Zelitsky," said Leah Rubin, ignoring my aunt, "if you want to earn a decent wage and stop being a learner . . ."

My mother stood up. Her face was flushed and she said in an excited voice, "Wait! Wait! I'm going to show you something," and she ran out of the room.

There was a strained silence, and then my aunt said bitterly, "How can she join the union? This year is a bad year, it's all we can do to pay the rent and put food in the children's mouths. My husband is making peanuts and we don't have an extra penny for anything."

My mother came back into the kitchen carrying some of her needlework from the old country. She spread out on the table some of the shirts she had made for me, her own wedding gown, and the one napkin from my trousseau.

"I can sew," said my mother. "I can do needlework good enough for lords and ladies. I'm no learner. See what I can do. See!"

"Mama," I cried, ashamed. "Nobody wants to see all those old things."

Leah picked up the shirts, then the wedding gown, and finally the napkin. Her fingers traced the flowers and scrolls.

"See!" my mother cried.

"Fanny, sit down," said my aunt. "You're all excited over nothing."

"It's very beautiful," said Leah. "It's a gift you have to be able to sew like that."

"But not anymore," said my mother, bursting into tears. "I can't do it anymore. I have no time. I'm too tired. No more."

"Drink a glass of tea, Fanny," said my aunt, "and please, miss, stop getting her so upset."

"But she should get upset," said Leah Rubin. "She can't go through life slaving away at a miserable job that she hates, working long hours that exhaust her, and bringing home a miserable wage. There has to be more in life than just that. She has to have time for herself to do what she likes. She has to have hope."

"She's not interested in bettering herself," I burst in. "She won't go to school and learn English. She doesn't read anything except the Jewish newspaper and she never wants to go anywhere."

But Leah was bending over my mother, saying, "Come, take a walk with me, Mrs. Zelitsky. A little fresh air will do you good."

"She's too tired," said my aunt.

"Just for a little while," Leah crooned. "We'll visit Hannah Schwartz, who lives right down the block. She's also in our shop."

My mother stood up and wiped the tears off her face. She gathered up all her needlework and carried it back to the parlor. When she returned, she was wearing her hat and coat.

"Don't stay out late," said my aunt. "You have to get up at six tomorrow."

"Good night, Mrs. Feldman. Good night, all," said Leah, taking my mother's arm.

"I don't like that young woman at all," said my aunt after they left. "I could see right away she's just a troublemaker."

Tanta Sadie had even more to say about the bad influence Leah Rubin was having on my mother when the next paycheck she handed over to my aunt was two dollars short.

"How foolish can you be?" said my aunt. "For two dollars you could buy yourself a pair of shoes or some new clothes."

My mother hung her head and said she was sorry but that night, after supper, she combed her hair, washed her face, and went to a union meeting with Leah Rubin.

My mother had joined the Ladies Waistmakers' Union, Local 25.

For a few more days my aunt continued grumbling but later that week, at supper, she seemed in particularly good spirits.

"I was talking to Mrs. Tannenbaum, downstairs front," she announced. "She was telling me about her brother, Joe Rosenberg, who has a garter belt business." She paused and looked at my mother, who was eating her soup. My mother continued eating so Tanta Sadie went on.

"He had a hard time in the beginning but now he's doing very well."

My aunt paused again and waited but my mother swallowed a mouthful of soup and put her spoon back into her bowl.

"So I said his wife must be very pleased and Mrs. Tannenbaum said he wasn't married. She said he never had a chance because he was so busy getting ahead. But now, and she said it, not me, Fanny, it was her idea . . . Fanny, are you listening to me?"

My mother stopped swallowing and looked blankly at my aunt.

"Mrs. Tannenbaum's brother, Joe Rosenberg," repeated my aunt patiently, "who has a successful garter belt business, is not married, and she said to me, 'Wouldn't it be a good idea for him to meet your pretty sister-in-law?' "

"I don't know," said my mother doubtfully.

"Don't be a fool," snapped my aunt. "It's going to hurt you just to say hello to the man? This Sunday, he's coming to his sister's for a dinner, and she wants you, and me too, we should just drop in later."

"I don't know . . . I told Leah I might go with her. She's going to visit some other girls in my shop and try to get them to join the union."

"Union, shmunion," said my aunt. "Just listen to me for a change."

So Sunday Mama got all dressed up in her one good dress and she and Tanta Sadie went downstairs to drop in on Mrs. Tannenbaum.

Shirley made me sit outside on the stoop with her earlier so we could watch for Mr. Rosenberg when he came. But so many strange men went in and out of the building that day it was hard to figure out which one he might have been.

My mother and Tanta Sadie stayed downstairs for a couple of hours. When they returned, my mother immediately went off to get out of her good dress. Tanta Sadie sat down at the kitchen table and smiled and nodded at Shirley and me. "Well, girls, we had a very nice visit. Mrs. Tannenbaum insisted that we have a glass of tea and a piece of her apple cake. I said, 'No, thank you. I'm fat enough.' And then Mr. Rosenberg, Mrs. Tannenbaum's brother, said he liked a woman to look like a woman so I said . . . Well, never mind what I said. But I had a glass of tea and so did Fanny, and Mr. Rosenberg told us one joke after another. Such a sense of humor . . . I nearly fell off my chair."

"Was he wearing a gray suit, Mama?" Shirley asked. "And did he bring a box of candy?"

"No, he had on a blue suit."

"Was he tall and good-looking?"

"Well, not exactly tall and good-looking. Handsome is as handsome does, I always say."

"Was he a little fat, old, bald man, Mama?"

"Of course not. He's maybe thirty, thirty-five, and not fat at all. A thin man with glasses."

"I didn't see a thin man with glasses, did you, Ruthie?" my cousin Shirley asked.

"No," I told her. "He must have come in before we went outside."

"Anyway, I laughed so hard, the tears were rolling down my face, and your mother . . ." My mother came out of the parlor dressed in her old clothes. "You know, Fanny, I think you should buy yourself a new hat, a straw one, and maybe some white gloves. The warm weather is beginning and you need a few things. I'll lend you the money."

My mother began to protest but Tanta Sadie interrupted. "So tell me—what did you think of Mr. Rosenberg?"

My mother wrinkled her forehead. "I didn't understand what he was saying," my mother said helplessly. "He talked so fast and everybody was laughing so loud."

"That was when he was talking in English, but when he talked in Yiddish?"

"He talked fast in Yiddish too."

"You'll get used to it." My aunt smiled and winked at me. Then she pulled me over to her and patted my hair. "Mr. Rosenberg is coming next Sunday to take you and your mother to the Metropolitan Museum of Art. He's a cultured man. He knows something about everything. But anyway, he's going to come after lunch and pick the two of you up. Then, after the museum, maybe you'll take a walk in Central Park. I never saw it myself but they say it's beautiful—like the real country. Ruthie, you should wear Shirley's pink dress with the pearl buttons and maybe, Fanny, I'll lend you my good shirtwaist with my cameo brooch to wear in the collar and my black straw hat. Too bad there isn't any time to go shopping but if everything goes all right . . ."

My mother blinked nervously and Tanta Sadie repeated severely, "If everything goes all right, Fanny, as I'm sure it will, we'll have plenty of time to go shopping for new clothes on another day."

Chapter 8

"My boss is a terrible man," said my mother at breakfast that Sunday morning. "Yesterday he fired Rosie Dubinsky because she missed a few days' work. She's a widow and her youngest child was sick with diphtheria. So what could she do? She had to take care of him. The boss has no heart."

"Ttt, Ttt, Ttt!" said my aunt as she spooned hot cereal into our plates.

"I wanted to tell him so but . . ."

"Just mind your own business, Fanny," said my aunt. "You're lucky you have a job."

"There was a young girl who spoke to us at the union meeting last week—a very young girl, maybe sixteen or seventeen," said my mother thoughtfully. "She stood up and spoke to us in Yiddish so I really understood and she said how her place went out on strike and the boss settled. Now they only work fifty-four hours a week and she doesn't have to pay for her needles when they break."

Tanta Sadie said she didn't want to listen to such nonsense but Uncle Barney said kindly, "Don't get your hopes up, Fanny. I've been a union man since I came to this country and I'm still working sixty-five hours a week when I work and getting paid starvation wages."

"You have to look out for yourself, Fanny," said Tanta Sadie, "and for your child. You have to consider Ruthie. It's not like she has a father . . ."

My mother's eyes filled with tears.

"I know, I know," said Tanta Sadie gently, patting my mother's hand, "but he's gone now and you have to start making plans. You know, Fanny, a lot of people think you're still very pretty. You're not twenty-six yet, not an old woman by any means. Of course, you've gotten too thin and you should use a little rouge and fix yourself up more. After all, you don't want to be working the rest of your life."

My mother looked startled.

"Yes," said my aunt. "It's time."

That was the day Mr. Rosenberg came to take us out to the Metropolitan Museum of Art. All morning long, Tanta Sadie coached my mother in the required etiquette and supervised her wardrobe.

"Don't tell Mr. Rosenberg you're tired all the time, and don't complain about your boss. Whatever you do, not one word about belonging to the union. Smile a little more. If he invites you and Ruthie to join him for some refreshments, just tell him, 'No, thank you.' If he asks you a second time, say it's not necessary because you and

Ruthie had a good lunch. But if he asks you a third time, then you can accept. You can always accept the third time. But don't order anything too expensive. You too, Ruthie. You hear?"

"Yes, Tanta Sadie."

She helped my mother dress, buzzing at her, patting a fold here, tucking in a bulge there. An hour before Mr. Rosenberg was due to arrive, my mother was dressed with her hat on, and seated stiffly but obediently in the kitchen, waiting.

"And try not to wrinkle your skirt when you sit down on the elevated train, Fanny. I notice you're not careful about pulling out your skirts on either side whenever you sit down."

"I will, I will," my mother promised.

Finally, when Mr. Rosenberg knocked at the door, Tanta Sadie whispered to my mother, "Go in one of the bedrooms. Don't be sitting here like you're waiting. Go!"

My mother hurried out of the room. Then my aunt opened the door. "Well, hello, Mr. Rosenberg. Very nice to see you. Come in. Come in. I think Fanny's getting ready. Come in. Sit down."

"Thank you, Mrs. Feldman," said Mr. Rosenberg. He was a thin man with bright eyes behind his glasses and he looked well-dressed in a dark suit and a black derby hat.

My aunt introduced Shirley and me. Mr. Rosenberg shook our hands and said it was a great pleasure for him to meet such beautiful young ladies. I liked him right away. We all sat down to wait for my mother and soon Mr. Rosenberg began asking us riddles.

"If a herring and a half cost a penny and a half, how much will twelve herrings cost?"

"Twelve and a half cents," said Shirley.

"No, twelve cents," I corrected her.

"I see I can't fool you," said Mr. Rosenberg, laughing.

"Oh, nobody can fool Ruthie," said Tanta Sadie. "She's so smart, the teachers can't get over her."

"How about this one," said Mr. Rosenberg. "A man wanted to get across a big river but there was no bridge and he didn't have a boat and he couldn't swim. What did he do?"

"I don't know," said Shirley.

"Me neither," said my aunt, looking toward the bedroom for my mother.

"Do you give up?"

"I don't give up," I said, trying to concentrate.

"Take your time," said Mr. Rosenberg.

"Come on, Ruthie, give up," said Shirley.

"All right," I said finally. "I give up."

"It's very simple," said Mr. Rosenberg. "He just went into a church and got a cross."

"I don't get it," said Shirley.

"A cross," Mr. Rosenberg explained. "You see, a cross and across. He got a cross so he could go across the river."

"Oh, Mr. Rosenberg," laughed Tanta Sadie and she stood up and said to me, "Ruthie dear, go tell your mama that Mr. Rosenberg is here."

The bedroom being right next to the kitchen, all of us, including Mr. Rosenberg, knew that my mother knew he was there.

My mother was sitting on my bed when I came in.

"Mama," I said, "we're all waiting for you."

"Oh," she said, "I didn't know when I was supposed to come out."

I took her hand and led her through the door. Mr. Rosenberg stood up and said, "Good day, Mrs. Zelitsky."

My mother muttered something in return and then looked nervously at my aunt.

"Well, it's a beautiful day," my aunt said heartily. "I hope you all have a good time."

The Metropolitan Museum of Art was up on Fifth Avenue and Eighty-second Street. We were going to take the Third Avenue Elevated train, the first time either my mother or I had ever been on it. But for two people who had ridden over half of Europe by train and come all the way across the Atlantic Ocean by boat, the Third Avenue El should not have made either of us nervous.

I certainly wasn't nervous as we walked up the stairs to the train platform.

"I always wanted to ride on the Third Avenue El," I told Mr. Rosenberg.

"I'm surprised you never have," he said, politely holding my mother by the elbow.

"Every place we go is in the neighborhood. And everybody we know lives close by."

"And you, Mrs. Zelitsky," he said, "how do you get to work in the morning?"

"I walk."

"And do you like your job?"

My mother hesitated. I suppose she was remembering my aunt's instructions about not complaining. "It's fine," she said quickly.

"What are your hours?"

"I work from eight to six, sometimes longer in the busy season, Monday through Saturday."

"Sometimes I have to keep my workers on Sundays too, when it's busy," said Mr. Rosenberg.

By this time we were standing on the train platform and my mother shrank back as far as she could from the edge. When the train came shrieking into the station, she gripped my hand so hard I said, "Mama, you're hurting me!" I pulled my hand away and Mr. Rosenberg smiled and led my mother into the train. "Don't worry, Mrs. Zelitsky," he said. "This is the most modern system of transportation in the whole world. You're safer in this train than in your own bed."

But when my mother looked out of the window and saw how the train was hurtling along forty or so feet above the ground, she grew white.

"Oiy! Oiy! It will fall down."

"No, no, Mrs. Zelitsky, don't worry. I've taken this train many times and I promise you there is absolutely no danger at all."

"Oiy! Vay iz mir!"

I watched my mother in disgust. Everybody on the train could hear her and see how frightened she was—like a real greenhorn. She was wringing her hands and tossing around, wrinkling up her skirt, exactly what Tanta Sadie had warned her against.

"Mama!" I whispered sharply. "Stop it!"

All the way up to Eighty-sixth Street, Mr. Rosenberg talked to my mother about the safety of the elevated trains and how they never, never fell off the tracks. My mother continued to wring her hands and groan. Her face grew paler and paler and finally she began to suck in deep gasps of air.

I recognized these symptoms. My mother was seasick.

By the time we reached Eighty-sixth Street, my mother had to be supported off the train by Mr. Rosenberg. Her legs were buckling under her and she looked around desperately for a public restroom.

Listening to the sounds of my mother's retching in the

washroom brought back memories of her on board the ship. Some of the women in the washroom made sympathetic noises but they smiled at each other in amusement. I felt humiliated.

"Wash your face, Mama," I said impatiently, when she emerged from the booth. "And fix your hair."

"I'm sorry," she said weakly. "I'm sorry."

"Mr. Rosenberg is waiting for us, Mama, so don't just stand there."

I helped her to straighten her clothes and hat and I shoved all her hairpins back into place. She washed her face but she was still pale and trembling when we rejoined Mr. Rosenberg.

"Maybe we should find a place where you could get a drink," he suggested.

"No, thank you," said my mother.

"A little seltzer might settle your stomach."

"I couldn't drink anything."

"Maybe Ruth would like something," he said, smiling at me.

I wasn't sure at this point whether I was supposed to say yes or no. My mother had refused twice and Aunt Sadie said she should accept the third time. But Mr. Rosenberg had not asked my mother a third time. He had asked me.

"I don't know," I said, confused.

Mr. Rosenberg took us into an ice-cream parlor and ordered some seltzer for my mother.

"You, Ruth, you order anything you want."

What I really wanted was an ice-cream soda or a sundae but they cost ten cents and Tanta Sadie said not to order anything too expensive.

"I'll have a lemon phosphate," I said. They cost only

five cents. But Mr. Rosenberg insisted that we both have ice-cream sodas. It was the first one I had ever tasted and I ate it slowly, sipping the delicious, cold chocolate soda and slowly digging out tiny pieces of ice cream with my long silver spoon.

My mother sat silently over her glass of seltzer, trying to avoid looking at us and our sodas.

"Try a little seltzer, Mrs. Zelitsky," Mr. Rosenberg urged gently. "You'll see, it will make you feel better."

My mother smiled weakly but shook her head.

We walked slowly toward the museum. My mother said nothing. Mr. Rosenberg supported her elbow but he talked to me. We talked about books and school and the opportunity to get ahead here in America. Mr. Rosenberg told me how he had come over to this country with holes in all his pockets and now he was his own boss. He only regretted, he said, that he had never finished school and hoped in the future he could take courses in art and literature. I liked him better and better the more he spoke and hoped that my mother would make a good impression, which hardly seemed likely considering her performance on the elevated train.

Wherever I looked there was something new to see. It was the first time I had ever been out of the Lower East Side and the first time I had ever seen such beautiful, elegant houses. There were sleek horses and fancy carriages moving along the streets and even some of those new automobiles. I gaped at them and Mr. Rosenberg laughed and told me he had actually ridden in one a couple of times.

Up on Fifth Avenue, the great museum stood with Central Park behind it. There were people moving up and down its stone steps, fashionable people who wore fine clothes and spoke to each other without a trace of an accent.

"Will they let us in?" I whispered to Mr. Rosenberg.

"The museum belongs to everybody," he said.

My mother refused to go inside. She said that all she wanted to do was sit outside in the fresh air.

"Come in for a little while," urged Mr. Rosenberg. "I'm sure you'll feel better once you see all the beautiful treasures inside."

My mother shook her head. She sank down on one of the stone benches at the entrance to the museum and said no.

"Mama," I urged, "Tanta Sadie will want to know what you saw. Tanta Sadie will be very interested in what you saw."

But even that could not budge her. She smiled a sick smile and said we should go and take our time and not worry about her.

So Mr. Rosenberg took me inside the museum and led me through the marble halls. He showed me Egyptian mummies and Roman statues and paintings from Italy in huge golden frames. Whenever he suggested that we return to my mother, I said, "Please, Mr. Rosenberg, a little longer. She'll be fine. Please."

We went in and out of the different galleries. We looked at knights in armor and tapestries that had hung on the walls of old castles. I forgot about my mother. I thought about me, moving through all the treasures in this splendid palace with its great staircase and magnificent stone pillars. The museum belonged to me just as much as it did to all the fashionable, elegant people because I was an American.

"We should go now, Ruth," said Mr. Rosenberg.

"Please, a little longer."

"Another time, Ruth. I will bring you another time, I promise. But your poor mama has been sitting by herself for over an hour."

My poor mama! Poor me to have such a mother!

She was still sitting in the same place when we came out but her face was less pale now and she managed a real smile. I looked away from her.

"So? Are you feeling better now, Mrs. Zelitsky?"

"Yes, I am. And did you have a nice time?"

"A lovely time, Mrs. Zelitsky. Your daughter is a very special, very intelligent young lady. She'll go far. You should be proud."

"Thank you," said my mother.

Mr. Rosenberg suggested we take a stroll in Central Park. When my mother saw the green lawns and the trees, she really cheered up. She even laughed a couple of times at some of the jokes Mr. Rosenberg told her, slowly, in Yiddish. We walked through the park and the sunshine felt warm on our heads. My mother breathed in the air and her cheeks turned rosy. Mr. Rosenberg talked mostly to me but he smiled whenever he looked at my mother's soft pink cheeks.

I thought to myself that I would always love my own papa best but I could get used to another father, one who took me up to the Metropolitan Museum of Art, and talked to me about books and school, and bought me ice-cream sodas.

But when Mr. Rosenberg said something about taking the Third Avenue El home, all my pleasant dreams for the future fell apart. My mother's face tightened and she refused to go.

"Just try," urged Mr. Rosenberg. "You're used to it now. You won't be so frightened going back."

My mother said no. She said that Mr. Rosenberg and I should take the El home and that she would walk. All he had to do was tell her where to go and show her the direction.

"You can't walk from here, Mrs. Zelitsky. We're miles and miles away from the Lower East Side."

My mother insisted. Mr. Rosenberg's face turned grim. "We'll have to take a cab then," he said. But my mother absolutely refused to go home on anything that had wheels. I was so ashamed I not only stopped looking at my mother, I stopped looking at Mr. Rosenberg too.

We walked. All the way home. It took hours and when we arrived home, there were blisters all over my toes and the soles of my feet were raw and swollen.

Tanta Sadie was sitting in the kitchen, an expectant look on her face as we came through the door.

"Well," she said, "did you have a good day? Did you eat supper out? I figured maybe he took you out to a restaurant, you were gone so long."

My mother threw an imploring look in my direction but I yelled out to my aunt, "She spoiled it all. She spoils everything. She got sick on the train and we had to walk all the way home. She ruined the whole day. She can't do anything right. She's just a greenhorn!"

Chapter 9

That morning in September of 1909 when we filed into our new classroom and found Miss Baxter standing at the desk, waiting for us, I thought she was the most beautiful woman I had ever seen in my whole life. Tall and slim, with cool blue/gray eyes, she stood stiffly waiting as we took our seats. Her soft brown hair was piled high on her head in an elegant pompadour and her skin was pale and delicate. As the girls continued filing into the room, she made a little grimace, took the long window pole, and opened all the top windows in the room although the morning was a cool one. She wore the usual shirtwaist and long skirt that most of our teachers wore. Nothing wrinkled or sagged and her long, slim neck rose gracefully inside her high, lacy collar.

She stood at the front of the room, inspecting us, her eyes moving slowly over the classroom. We waited for her to speak but she said nothing until all the rustling and moving had stopped and the room froze into silence. Then, in a cool, low voice, she introduced herself and told us she would be our teacher for the rest of the 6A term.

Her eyes continued their examination, resting on each of the fifty girls in her class. When her eyes reached mine, I smiled and nodded to reassure her that I could be counted upon as an ally. Nothing flickered in response on her face as her eyes moved on. Celia Holstein, who wore a stiffly starched, new dress that day, was selected to hold the flag. In the days that followed other girls were selected to hold the flag but never me. Teacher said she generally picked the neatest girl in the class. I knew that my own clothes were always clean and neatly pressed. But I hadn't had a new dress since the spring and it did seem to me that Teacher admired new dresses just about as much as she admired cleanliness and neatness.

"I need a new dress," I told Tanta Sadie. I didn't want to tell her the real reason so I said, "My old ones are getting tight across my chest, and see, Tanta Sadie, the sleeves on this one don't even cover my wrists."

"I know, I know," Tanta Sadie agreed. "And Joey needs a new pair of shoes and so do you and Shirley. But with shoes costing two dollars a pair these days, who can afford it. You know Uncle Barney's been out of work for a month. Wait until he finds a new job, then we'll buy you a dress. Meanwhile, maybe you can wear that blue dress that's too small on Shirley?"

"But I'm just as tall as Shirley."

My aunt shook her head and said that Uncle Barney

was out looking for a job that morning. He had heard that there was a big Ladies' Cloak and Suit Company on Division Street that needed experienced cutters.

But the slack season had already started and my uncle could not find a job as a cutter. Finally, just until things improved, he took a job as a presser in a tailor shop, making about half of his accustomed wage.

Tanta Sadie grumbled about making ends meet, Uncle Barney complained bitterly about his job, and my mother's eyes shone every time she came home from a union meeting.

"The bad times are coming to an end," she said. "Tonight the organizer told us that the union is growing stronger every day. Workers aren't afraid to stand up for their rights. More and more strikes are breaking out."

"Don't be a fool," Tanta Sadie snapped. "You're spending too much time with that Leah Rubin. She's making you crazy."

"Not crazy," said my mother. "She's making me feel good."

"Feel good?" repeated Tanta Sadie. "Good when we have to struggle just to pay the rent and put a little food on the table? This is the worst year we've had since we first came to this country and you feel good?"

"I can't help it," said my mother apologetically. "I used to feel, after Shmuel died and there was nothing but work, work, work, I used to feel if it wasn't for Rifka, I'd just as soon be dead."

"Fanny," Tanta Sadie cried, "to talk like that in front of the children! Go outside and play, Shirley, Ruth . . . go outside."

"It's all right, Sadie," said my mother. "I only felt like that because I thought it would never change. That I'd always have to slave away and never have time to do what I wanted. I used to dream about the old country, about my mother and father, and how happy I was there. I hated America. But now it's different."

"Don't get your hopes up," my Uncle Barney muttered. "Some things will never change."

"But why not?" insisted my mother. "Last week, another shop signed up with the union and now the workers there only have to work fifty-four hours a week. Imagine what I could do if I only worked fifty-four hours. I could have time to be with Rifka. I could start working on her trousseau. I could walk in the park . . ."

"Not Central Park," I reminded her. "Not anywhere you had to take a train."

My mother blinked.

"Very nice daydreams," retorted my aunt. "But meanwhile Ruthie needs some clothes. The other day she came to me and showed me how tight her dress is across the chest. I don't want to upset you, Fanny, but you have to stop daydreaming and think a little more about your responsibilities. Ruthie's growing up. She needs clothes. She needs . . ."

My aunt listed all the things I needed and my mother's head drooped lower and lower.

"You should keep away from that Leah Rubin," said my aunt. "She's just a troublemaker."

Miss Baxter, my teacher, didn't like troublemakers either. Those girls who passed notes and giggled and asked permission to leave the room, Teacher said would never amount to anything in this world. She said all of us had to learn self-control if we expected to be respected in the future. She said we were very lucky to live in a country that gave us all the opportunity to improve our position in life and to become worthwhile citizens. America, Teacher said, was a great melting pot in which the humblest person through hard work and self-control could become a great American.

I agreed with everything Teacher said and I strove to show her. I did my homework every night. If Teacher asked us to write a composition using two sides of the paper, I often wrote one on two pages using four sides. Sometimes I even wrote two. In arithmetic, I was already doing percentages when the rest of the class still struggled with fractions and in history, my hand was always the first to go up.

"Ruth Zelitsky, please stay after class today," said Miss Baxter one day.

I shivered with pleasure and looked around me at my less fortunate classmates. Sure enough, jealousy was plainly written across many faces. Miss Baxter had been slow to single me out but sooner or later, recognition always came for me. I had admired all of my teachers and they always favored me. But I adored Miss Baxter. When she walked up and down the rows, looking down over our shoulders at our work, and I could hear the soft swish of her skirt and smell the fragrance of her perfume, it seemed to me I was the luckiest of creatures. She became my model for the perfect woman. I tried to stand up straight as she did, speak softly and distinctly as she did, and raise my eyebrows in amazement when something foolish was said. When I looked at my face in the mirror, so much like my mother's face, with its round red cheeks, its dark eyes, and curly hair, I despaired.

"Yes, Miss Baxter," I said, standing near her chair, after the others had gone.

My imagination had exploded with possibilities. Perhaps Teacher would ask me to hold the flag every morning from now on. Perhaps she would ask me to fill the inkwells or stay after school to sort papers. I had visions of helping her carry books home and being invited into a house something like the Metropolitan Museum of Art, filled with art treasures and gleaming chandeliers.

Miss Baxter's cool eyes rested on me. She drew her chair back a little, and said, "Ruth, I really must have a few words with you."

"Yes, Teacher?" I said eagerly. Perhaps she wished to compliment me on the two compositions I had just handed in on "A Humorous Incident" or on the map of South America I had drawn for her before it was even due.

"Ruth," said Miss Baxter, frowning, "you are becoming something of a problem."

"I am, Teacher?" I cried.

"Yes. I know you are anxious to please, Ruth, but you really must learn not to be so pushy."

"Pushy, Teacher?"

"Yes, Ruth. You continually demand extra attention and I must tell you that it is a very unpleasant trait in a girl your age."

"But what did I do?"

"You continually force yourself on my notice," said Miss Baxter sternly, her beautiful forehead wrinkled in annoyance. "Your hand is always the first up and it continues wagging even after someone else has been selected. You do not follow instructions as you should. When I ask for one composition, I do not want you to do two. When I ask you to do one set of problems in your arithmetic book, I do not want you to go on to the next set. I'm afraid you show off too much, Ruth, and you do not respect my wishes."

"But I do respect your wishes, Miss Baxter. I only want to please you."

"Well, then," said Miss Baxter, her forehead smoothing out again, "it should be very simple. Just don't push too hard. It's very unbecoming in a young lady. I know you are there and I also know you are a hard worker and an intelligent girl. But there are forty-nine other girls in the class. I simply do not have the time to give you all of my attention."

My head drooped, and I stood there looking at my shoes. It was very quiet in the room. I could hear myself breathing and I wondered if I could hold back the tears that were pushing into my eyes.

Miss Baxter's soft hand raised my chin so that my eyes were looking into hers. She examined me curiously for a moment and then she said, "It's self-control, Ruth." Her voice was kindly. "I know that in some countries people are encouraged to speak up boldly and to show all their feelings. But believe me, dear, and this is for your own good, in this country, people respect good manners, and good manners means self-control. Do you understand?"

"Yes, Miss Baxter."

"Very good. I'm sure we're going to get along very well now. So run along and don't forget what I told you."

"Yes, Miss Baxter," I whispered and fled from the room.

Two of my classmates were waiting for me outside.

"What did Teacher want?" one of them asked jealously. "Is she going to let you hold the flag?"

But I just looked at them coolly and raised my eyebrows and hurried away before they could see me cry.

Chapter 10

Maybe if my father had been alive I could have talked to him about Miss Baxter. I think he would have consoled me for the suffering her rebuke had caused me. I think he would have taken me into his lap and let me cry it all out against his chest while he patted my shoulder and rocked me in his arms and told me not to worry, it would all work out.

Then, I think, he would have advised me to take Miss Baxter's words to heart and try to do what she asked. After all, she was a teacher. She knew what was best for little immigrant girls who wanted to grow up to be good Americans even if their papas did consider them perfect just the way they were.

I missed my father very much that fall. Tanta Sadie

worried and grumbled and my cousin Shirley quarreled with me all the time.

"She started it, Mama. She said I dropped her library book in the street."

"You did drop it in the street. In a big puddle, and you did it on purpose because you said I was showing off, carrying such a big book."

"I did not. But you were showing off. You're always showing off."

"I am not, and you're going to have to pay for it."

"I am not."

"You will too or I'll tell."

"Tattletale! Tattletale!"

"Out!" yelled Tanta Sadie. "Both of you, out!"

Shirley stayed mad at me. She began playing more and more with Roslyn Berger who lived around the corner, and she hardly ever asked me to come along. At night, when we slept together in the big bed in the bedroom, she just turned away and stopped whispering to me as we always used to do.

I missed Shirley's friendship more than she missed mine. She had many friends but I had only her. Some nights I tried talking to her back. I tried to act as if nothing had happened between us. Sometimes I tried to tell her about Miss Baxter. Once I even started crying but in between my sobs I could hear Shirley's deep, even breathing. She had fallen asleep.

There was nobody I could talk to. Certainly not my mother. She went regularly to union meetings now and always returned home with a shining rosy face and a desperate look in her eyes as if she was bursting. She needed to talk to somebody too, but she knew better than to try telling Tanta Sadie or Uncle Barney about her union activities. Sometimes she tried talking to me but I wasn't interested. All I was interested in was making up with Shirley and pleasing Miss Baxter.

I tried all the time to please Miss Baxter. I sat stiffly and quietly in my seat. I followed her instructions to the letter. I never raised my hand until two or three other hands were up, and mine was always the first to drop when Teacher called on somebody else. But still, I could not elicit any praise or approving smiles from Miss Baxter.

Not that anyone else in the class was favored. Teacher had no pets. She kept all of us at a distance and after a few weeks of school, most of the girls in the class began to grumble.

"Teacher is mean."

"Teacher is stuck-up."

"Teacher thinks she's better than anybody else."

"She *is* better than anybody else," I cried in her defense. "She's beautiful and intelligent and she's trying to teach us how to behave like proper young ladies."

"Teacher doesn't even like you."

"She does. She does like me," I cried. "In this country, people don't show all their feelings like greenhorns. They have self-control."

One morning, late in November, when I was wearing my old blue and red striped dress, Teacher's eyes settled on me.

"Ruth," she said, "you may hold the flag today."

I knew it was not because of my dress, which was too old and faded. What had I done I wondered as I stood up as straight and stiff as I could, holding the flag while my classmates recited the Pledge of Allegiance. Teacher's hand rested lightly on my shoulder for a moment when it was over. I knew Teacher was pleased.

After I sat down, she said to the class, "I want to talk to you, girls, about the compositions you all handed in the other day on 'A Good Citizen.' I am going to return them to you, and I want you to look over the comments. Some of you, whose papers were dirty or carelessly written, will do them over again. I am not at all pleased with the penmanship in this class in general. Please practice your exercises at home.

"In terms of content, I realize that none of you are likely to become distinguished literary figures. I am hoping, however, that you will be able to write clear, understandable English by the time you finish grammar school. I wonder why it seems so difficult for most of you to express even the simplest thought on paper. Most of the compositions were totally illiterate, one or two were barely passable, and only one was acceptable. Ruth Zelitsky, you may come up and read your paper to the class."

I tried to walk slowly, to hide my joy, to keep the triumph out of my voice as I read.

A Good Citizen

A good citizen finds many ways to serve his country. We hope that when our country needs us we will be ready. In times of war, our lives must be placed at our country's disposal. We must think back to our heroes and martyrs of the past. We must remember Nathan Hale whose brave words on the scaffold, "I only regret that I have but one life to give for my country," still should be the inspiration for all of us.

We need not wait until we grow up to show

our country how much we love her. In many small ways we can demonstrate that love and devotion. We must obey the laws of our land. They have been made for our good. Those children who spit on the streets or steal an apple from a pushcart are not good citizens. They may think that a little crime is not the same as a big one, like murder or arson. But little steps can become big steps and an immoral child will become an immoral man or woman.

As children we need to learn all about our great country and how we best may serve her. We need to respect our teachers who serve as our guides and to understand that their criticism is for our own good. We need to learn self-control and obedience so that one day we can make our country proud of us.

"Ugh!" I could hear Helen Fogelman grunt when I had finished. A few of the other girls in the class were also making the kind of face you make when something smells bad.

"You may sit down, Ruth," said Miss Baxter. "I think Ruth's composition is somewhat clumsy in its sentence construction and the language is not striking. But her thoughts are clearly expressed and that is essentially all I expect from you."

It was high praise from Miss Baxter, and I arrived home from school more joyful than I had been in a long time.

"Teacher asked me to read my composition to the class," I announced at supper.

Tanta Sadie dished out bowls of bean and barley soup

and complained about the bones the butcher had given her to make the soup.

"He says he gives away bones only to his customers who buy meat. So I said to him, 'Mr. Beckerman, *Mr. Ganuff*, how many years have I been buying meat from you? How many years have you been overcharging me for pieces of meat that were all fat and gristle? Just because these past couple of months I haven't been able to buy as much as usual and you haven't been able to cheat me as much as usual, you dare to argue over a few bones, and not even marrow bones at that!' "

"Teacher said mine was the only good composition in the whole class."

My mother was watching me, her eyes very bright.

"Rifka," she said.

"Call me Ruth," I told her. "What is it?"

"Rifka . . . I mean, Ruth . . . do you know where Cooper Union is?"

"What's that?" Tanta Sadie wanted to know.

"Nothing, nothing," my mother said hastily, but later, after supper, she drew me into the parlor and showed me a flyer that said a big meeting from Local 25 would be held that night at Cooper Union on Cooper Square to discuss a general strike.

"Rifka darling," my mother pleaded. "Please. I don't know how to go there, and most of the girls in my shop are going by train. It's not too far to walk but I don't know the way. Please, Rifka, will you come with me?"

"Does Tanta Sadie know?" I asked her.

"No, and I don't want to tell her. She gets upset over nothing these days."

"I have homework to do, Mama."

"Rifka," said my mother, and her voice was very

serious. "I have to go to that meeting." She put her hand on my arm and looked into my face.

I hesitated. But the day had been filled with pleasure for me. I could afford to be generous.

"All right, Mama," I said. "I'll go with you tonight but don't expect me to do it again."

"Where are the two of you going?" Tanta Sadie asked suspiciously as we left the house.

"Just taking a little walk," my mother murmured. "We'll be back soon."

On the way over, my mother tried to talk to me about the union. She explained that several strikes had broken out that fall in the shirtwaist industry to protest the terrible working conditions in the sweatshops. Some of them had been settled favorably for the workers, and now the union thought it might be time for a general strike to improve conditions for all shirtwaist workers.

I decided to tell my mother about Miss Baxter.

"She's so beautiful, Mama, like a lady in a painting. She's tall and her hair is light brown with a beautiful, soft wave in it, and her face is perfect. You should see her clothes, Mama. They never wrinkle and she has different shirtwaists that she wears for each day of the week."

"I'm glad you have a nice teacher, Rifka," said my mother.

"She is the best one I ever had," I told her, "and the most beautiful."

"Maybe someday I can meet her."

I looked sideways at my mother, at her old winter coat and hat with its faded ribbons. My mother's shoes were scuffed and cracked across the toes. What would Teacher think of my mother, I wondered, but I knew the answer even before I asked the question.

"They have one day a term when parents can visit the classroom and talk to the teacher but it's during the day when you're working," I told her, "so I don't think you'll be able to come."

My mother sighed and said one day she knew there would be time to do other things besides just work. Maybe if there was a strike and it was successful, she said, we could spend more time together. "Like we used to, Rifka," she said. "Remember, in the old country, the way we used to roll around in the fields together?"

I looked away, embarrassed.

"And you know, Rifka, as soon as I have a little more time, I'm going to start on that tablecloth and napkins for your trousseau. You'll see, Rifka, I really will."

"Call me Ruth," I told her.

At Cooper Union, there were thousands of people trying to get through the door. Leah Rubin was acting as an usher and she squeezed my mother and me into the big assembly room where people were jammed together like sardines. Most of them were women and girls, young ones, some not much older than myself. They were dressed up in their best clothes. Few of them looked as shabby as my mother. In front of us, two young women sat, wearing large hats with feathers that rose high in the air and blocked our view of the speakers' platform at the front of the hall.

The president of the union began to speak and one by one, other speakers rose and addressed the crowd. Mr. Samuel Gompers, president of the American Federation of Labor, arrived in the hall and when he was introduced, everybody stood up and applauded and cheered.

"Who was that?" asked my mother. "I didn't understand."

"That was Mr. Samuel Gompers of the American Federation of Labor," I told her.

"What is he saying?" my mother asked as he began speaking in English.

"He says you shouldn't cheer for him. He would rather you cheered for the union and your cause."

"And what's he saying now?"

"Shh! Shh!" said the people all around us.

"See!" I whispered to my mother. "If you would go to school and learn English, you would know what Mr. Gompers is saying."

One after another, different prominent people stood up to discuss conditions in the sweatshops and whether or not it would be advisable to strike. Some said yes. Some said no. Most said maybe but . . . My mother wiggled and squirmed in her seat, trying to peer through the little spaces between feathers and hats to see speakers whom she could not understand.

The hours passed and the speakers grew more and more boring.

"Mama, let's go home, I'm tired," I whispered.

"A few minutes more, Rifka. Please. Just a few minutes!"

"You can't understand what they're saying anyway. And it's boring. They're never going to decide on anything."

The speakers droned on and on and the audience began to grow restless. Suddenly, a small, young girl in the audience jumped to her feet and demanded the floor.

"That's Clara Lemlich," somebody said.

The young girl ran up to the speakers' platform and cried out in Yiddish, "I am a working girl. I am tired of listening to speakers who talk in general terms. What we are here for is to decide whether or not we shall or shall not strike. I offer a resolution that a general strike be declared NOW!"

"Yes, yes!" my mother shouted and before I could stop her she jumped to her feet. All around her other people rose from their seats, waving hats, scarves, umbrellas—anything they could find.

"Yes, yes! Strike! Strike!" came from thousands of voices. For five minutes, at least, the shouting and cheering went on. The chairman pounded his gavel again and again before he could make himself heard. He asked for a second to the resolution. Again the huge audience rose and yelled a unanimous second.

"Do you mean it?" the chairman said. "Do you mean it in absolute faith? Will you take the old, Jewish oath?"

Thousands of hands rose with the response. "If I turn traitor to the cause I now pledge, may this hand wither from the arm I now raise."

All around me people hugged and kissed one another. "Tomorrow," they cried. "Tomorrow!"

"What are you going to tell Tanta Sadie?" I asked my mother as we began walking home.

My mother's face was radiant.

"Did you see her, Rifka? Did you see that little wisp of a girl, Clara Lemlich? She's still in her teens but a real leader. She's been in a strike already and some thugs beat her up. That's what they told me. But she wasn't afraid. Not her. Did you see the way she stood up there in front of all those people and called for a strike? She wasn't afraid."

"But Mama, what are you going to tell Tanta Sadie?"

"She's an inspiration to all of us." My mother's face wrinkled as she concentrated.

"So, Mama?"

"I just don't know, Rifka, how you're supposed to dress on a picket line. You noticed how everybody was so dressed up tonight. Do you think I should wear my good dress? Maybe Sadie would loan me her hat with the nose veil."

"Mama, I asked you a question."

"What, Rifka? What did you ask me?"

"I asked you what you were going to tell Tanta Sadie?"

My mother's face grew pale. "You tell her, Rifka. She never gets mad at you."

"No, I'm not going to tell her. It wasn't my idea, and Tanta Sadie isn't going to like it. She's going to get mad, Mama."

"Oiy vay!"

"I don't think you should go out on strike, Mama. I think you just better forget the whole thing."

"But Rifka, I just swore an oath. You heard me, Rifka. I can't break an oath."

I shrugged my shoulders and as we continued walking home, my mother pleaded with me to break the news of the strike to my aunt. Of course, I refused.

Chapter 11

"I was the first one in my shop to get up," said my mother proudly. "The day the strike started, we all went in to work and sat down by our machines and watched each other. I watched Leah and she watched Rose, and Rose was looking at Annie. Nobody wanted to be the first to get up. We were all afraid of the boss. We thought maybe the boss would remember who started it. Then the foreman began giving us our bundles of work, and I got up and put on my hat. I didn't know if anybody else was going to get up and I was scared. 'Where are you going, Fanny?' said the foreman. 'Sit down and do your work.' But then Rose got up and put on her hat and then Leah, then all of them. You could hear a big crack as a bunch of them suddenly jumped up together. Down in the street, other girls were pouring down from their shops and we all hugged and kissed and cried."

My mother had never dressed as well as she did during the strike. Her shirtwaists crackled with starch and she brushed her skirts and old coat until they were free from the smallest speck of dust. She began to tuck "rats" into her hair to make it stay up in a full pompadour, and she rouged her cheeks, and put powder on her nose.

"Like you're going to a fancy wedding," said my aunt bitterly.

One day she came home wearing a new hat.

"You went out and bought yourself a new hat?" my aunt cried.

"No, no, no," said my mother. "Leah and I got tired of wearing our own hats so we exchanged for one day. Maybe," she giggled, "Helen Zimmerman and I will wear each other's hats tomorrow."

"Like a party!" snapped my aunt. "Like a real party! Well, go ahead and enjoy yourself, Fanny. It doesn't matter if the rest of us are starving to death."

My mother tried to look contrite. She tried to keep her face solemn in response to my aunt's anger.

"When the strike is over," she said meekly, "I'll be making more money, Sadie. I'll pay you back for everything."

"When the strike is over," answered my aunt. "I just hope we'll all be alive."

My mother began singing again. When she wasn't singing, she was humming. Early in the morning, when Tanta Sadie slammed the bread on the table and served us all our hot coffee, you could hear the songs humming inside my mother's throat.

"I'm learning some new English songs, Rifka," my

mother told me. "We sing all the time on the picket line. We teach each other songs. I sing all my Yiddish songs and some of the Italian girls sing Italian songs and we all sing 'Hold the Fort.' Listen, Rifka."

> *We meet today in freedom's cause*
> *And raise our voices high,*
> *We'll join our hands in union strong*
> *To battle or to die.*
> *Hold the fort for we are coming,*
> *Union girls be strong,*
> *Side by side we battle onward,*
> *Victory will come.*

As the strike continued into December, Tanta Sadie's temper grew increasingly short. She stopped speaking directly to my mother, and she yelled at the children for nothing. Even at me.

"You can take your nose out of the book, Princess Ruth, and run to the store for me. For what your mother's paying, I'm not going to be your slave anymore."

There were no pennies for candy and we began eating potatoes and herring for most of our suppers.

"It's my mother's fault," I said to Shirley. "If she was working, we wouldn't be so short of money."

Shirley wasn't mad at me for the time being. She thought the strike was exciting and she wanted to go down to Greene Street, where my mother's shop was, to see the pickets.

"Tanta Sadie won't like it."

"We won't tell her. Let's go after school. She'll think we're out playing."

After school, Shirley and I walked down to Greene

Street. All along the way, there were other shops that were being struck. Young women, dressed up in their best clothes, for the most part, milled around in front of the shops while policemen shouted at them to keep moving. Even before we reached Greene Street, we could hear the singing, and even above the sound of many voices came my mother's high, lovely voice in Yiddish.

> *This is the way a tailor sews,*
> *This is how he really sews,*
>
> *He sews and sews the whole week long,*
> *And earns a penny and a song;*
>
> *A tailor sews to earn his bread,*
> *But gets the misery instead.*
>
> *A year ago we all worked late.*
> *Never again! From eight to eight.*
>
> *But the union set us straight,*
> *We work no more from eight to eight.*

My mother was walking up and down in a line of pickets. She had her arm around another young woman and both of them were singing at the top of their lungs. They sang one song after another and tried not to listen to a group of tough-looking men who stood off to one side, taunting them. Every so often, one of them would stick out his foot and trip one of the pickets or push her against another girl. A few policemen who were standing close by didn't seem to notice.

"Tanta Fanny, Tanta Fanny!" Shirley yelled out. "Over here!"

My mother looked around until she spotted us. Then she smiled and nodded and broke out of the ranks to join us.

"Shirley and Rifka!" Her cheeks were very red and she smiled a broad smile.

"Tanta Fanny, who are those men who keep bothering the pickets?"

"The strikebreakers," said my mother angrily. "The bosses hire them and the police are on their side. They pick on us and push us and hit us and the police never notice."

As we were talking, one of the strikebreakers tripped a picket and she fell heavily to the ground. The girl next to her cried out, "Bully!" and he slapped her hard across her face. Two other girls ran over and grabbed his arm and, suddenly, there were four policemen surrounding the two girls and handcuffing them.

"But it wasn't their fault," Shirley cried. "It was the man."

The man was standing, watching the scene, and laughing as the two girls were led away.

"It isn't fair," Shirley cried.

"No," sighed my mother, "it isn't fair. Every day they arrest more and more girls for nothing. But we're not afraid. There are twenty thousand of us and they can't arrest us all."

My mother hurried back to her co-workers and soon her voice rose bright and clear above the others.

"I don't know what's gotten into her," I told Shirley. "I think she's gone crazy."

Miss Baxter said the pickets were a disgrace to this country and to God. She read us an article in the paper which told how Judge Olmstead, when he sentenced a striker, said to her, "You are on strike against God and Nature whose law it is that man shall earn his bread by the sweat of his brow. You are on strike against God."

She said it was a disgrace how thousands of young women betrayed their own sex by acting in such an immoral fashion. It was bad enough, Teacher said, when men took to the streets and promoted violence, but for women to behave like wild animals was a sign of the wickedness of the times. Never before in the history of this country had twenty thousand women gone out on strike. She warned us that unless people exercised self-control and showed obedience to authority, this country and all it stood for would be destroyed.

I was not the only one who squirmed miserably in her seat. There were other girls in the class whose mothers, sisters, aunts, cousins . . . were out there picketing in the streets too. But I think my own humiliation was the greatest. Especially since Miss Baxter had begun to distinguish me more and more in unmistakable ways. Only yesterday, she had commented on the improvement in my posture, and last week, she had asked me to water the plants for the rest of the term. What would she think of me if she discovered my mother was not only a striker, but the one with the loudest singing voice as well?

"The noise, the racket those people make," Teacher said. "They chant and shriek and create such a din, I wonder their own eardrums don't burst."

Christmas was coming. Even for a Jewish child living in the Lower East Side, the snap and tingle of Christmas was in the air. Teacher taught us Christmas carols— "Silent Night" and "O Come, All Ye Faithful." We drew big green Christmas trees with red and blue decorations and Teacher promised us a party in school the last day before the holidays began.

I needed a Christmas present to give Miss Baxter. Last year, Tanta Sadie had given me some money to buy a box of embroidered handkerchiefs for my teacher. The year before, my own papa had paid for a satin pincushion. But this year, for Miss Baxter, I needed something much more beautiful and elegant than anything I had given my previous teachers.

Tanta Sadie never stopped complaining about money all through December. My mother pawned her wedding ring, a pair of brass candlesticks she had brought with her from Europe, her wedding gown, and all her embroidered linens except the one napkin from my trousseau.

"Give up this crazy strike," my aunt yelled at her, "before we all starve to death."

I decided not to ask my aunt for money to buy Miss Baxter a Christmas present. But I asked my mother. She looked down at her hands without a wedding ring. All the scabs and sores from where the needles had punctured her skin were just about healed in the weeks since the strike began.

"It has to be something special," I told her. "For forty cents I can get her imported perfume in a beautiful cut-glass bottle."

"I only wish you could."

"Even for twenty-nine cents, I could get her a pompadour comb with little jeweled stars."

"Rifka, darling, there is no money. Not a cent."

"I *have* to buy her something," I shouted at my mother. "I have to. Hennie Levitt is getting her a manicure set in a red velvet box and Marsha Cohen is buying her a pair of gloves."

"Rifka," said my mother, "when the strike is over . . ."

"That's all you think about," I yelled at her, "the strike, the strike, the strike . . . All you're interested in is the strike. You don't care about me or Miss Baxter, who is the best teacher I have ever had. If Papa only knew . . ."

I ran out of the room and put my fingers in my ears when my mother tried to console me.

I was determined to buy Miss Baxter a gift, and not just any gift.

The days grew colder and a little snow fell. The hot sweet potato man wrapped himself up in his scarf and the smells of his roasting potatoes filled the air. Only three days remained until the final day of school before the Christmas holidays began. I still had nothing to give Miss Baxter.

That night, my mother did not come home for supper.

"She's busy with her union friends," complained my aunt. "One of these days, she'll just forget where she lives altogether."

At eight o'clock, Leah Rubin came to our house.

"If you're looking for Fanny," my aunt snapped at her, "she's not here."

"No, no, Mrs. Feldman, I know where she is and I'm afraid you're going to be upset."

"She's not in the hospital?" said my aunt.

"No—not in the hospital."

"So where is she?"

"She's in jail."

My first thought was that Miss Baxter must never find

out. If Teacher knew my mother was in jail, she would never let me water the plants, much less hold the flag.

"My God," yelled my aunt, "what did she do?"

"She didn't do anything," said Leah. "It happened a few hours ago. All day long she'd been on the picket line, walking up and down, singing, laughing, keeping everybody's spirits up. She really is a wonderful woman, Mrs. Feldman. Everybody respects her so much."

"So what did she do?"

"At six o'clock, some of the scabs began leaving the shop, escorted by those tough strikebreakers who hang around and torment us all day long. Fanny knew one of the scabs—a girl who used to work next to her in the shop. She called out her name—Dora. 'Dora!' she said, 'How can you do this to us? How can you betray your own friends? Come, Dora! Come join us and be one of us. We'll help you. Come!' The woman hesitated. You could see she felt bad. She looked at Fanny, and Fanny smiled at her and held out her hand. Then, one of the strikebreakers began beating her and kicking her and the police rushed in and arrested her."

"My God!" cried my aunt. "Such a disgrace!"

"It's not a disgrace," said Leah. "You should be proud."

"Get out!" shrieked my aunt. "Troublemaker! If it wasn't for you, she'd still be a decent, honest woman and not a jailbird."

The next day, my mother, along with some of the other strikers, was sentenced to a week in the workhouse on Blackwell's Island. My uncle had gone down to court and told us that the judge had said he was going to make an example of people who disturbed the peace and promoted hate and violence. If they protested an honest day's work for an honest day's wage, let them see how they liked to toil in the workhouse for nothing.

"Poor Fanny!" said my uncle.

"Poor me and you and the children," said my aunt. "Such a disgrace she's brought on the family. It's a good thing Sam didn't live to see this day."

My uncle said, "There were all kinds of people down at the court, on the side of the strikers. Rich people, too, society people even. I've been in strikes before but none like this. Usually we lost and everybody was against us. But this time, twenty thousand girls, young girls without any real experience, are running the strike. They don't even have any trained leaders. Every day they go out and every day some of them get arrested. But it's different, Sadie. This time, people are on their side. Those people in court, those rich people, put up bail and some of them even join the girls on the picket lines. I don't know, Sadie, maybe this really will be the beginning . . ."

"Don't you start in now," said my aunt. "That's all we need is for you to go out on strike."

"Even the newspapers are on their side. Did you hear about the article in the *Tribune* yesterday?"

"I don't want to hear about it, Barney, and you can be sure I'll give Fanny a piece of my mind when she comes home."

My aunt said if I didn't want to go to school for a few days, if I felt the humiliation was too great since everybody in the neighborhood was sure to know, then I could stay home. But Friday was the Christmas party, and on Friday, I was going to give Miss Baxter a present for Christmas. I had no choice. There was only one gift I could give her, only one beautiful thing that still belonged to me.

Chapter 12

"It belongs to me," I said to myself as I wrapped it up in a piece of brown paper and tied it with one of my old hair ribbons that didn't look too worn. "It's mine, not hers. She only made it but it belongs to me."

I tried to work myself up into a fury about my mother. The greater my anger, the better I felt about giving Teacher the one remaining napkin from my trousseau.

"She always said she would make me a tablecloth and other napkins but we've been in this country nearly two and a half years and she never even started. She doesn't care about me. All she cares about is her union. She won't even notice if it's gone."

I hid the gift inside my books so Shirley wouldn't see.

When she asked me what I had decided to give Miss Baxter, I just shrugged my shoulders.

"Never mind," Shirley said as we walked to school that morning. She wasn't giving her teacher anything either, she said, and besides, "Teachers always tell their classes that they'd rather not receive gifts. '

"But they don't mean it," I told her

"Listen, Ruthie." Shirley said, ' don't feel so bad about your mother."

I turned my face away and didn't answer. Jailbird! Jailbird! I said to myself, trying to keep the anger blazing.

"My teacher said she has a lot of admiration for the strikers."

"She did?"

"She said if she was one of those girls, working under inhuman conditions and being paid starvation wages, she would be out picketing too."

"If it was your mother in jail, you wouldn't like it," I told her.

"Oh, I don't know," said Shirley "It's sort of romantic —like being Joan of Arc."

"I don't think so. I think it's a disgrace A decent woman shouldn't be fighting with the police in the street. That's not the way a real lady behaves."

"Pooh! Pooh!" said Shirley. "There you go again, acting like you're better than anybody else. Aren't you even sorry for your mother?"

"No," I said. "I'm just ashamed of her."

"Well," Shirley said. "I'm not and when she gets out, I'm going to tell her so."

"I probably won't even talk to her," I said.

Miss Baxter's desk was piled high with Christmas presents. Some were in brown paper like mine, while others were wrapped in colored tissue paper and tied with bright ribbons. Teacher's face grew pink as the stacks of presents rose and she shook her head and said she wished her students had not bothered. Nobody could concentrate on work that day. In the afternoon, Miss Baxter passed out red and white candies and sugar cookies. We sang our Christmas carols and then Teacher read us parts of *A Christmas Carol* by Charles Dickens.

I listened hungrily as Teacher described the dinner at Bob Cratchit's house. I could smell the goose with its rich stuffing, fragrant with sage and onions. I helped Peter Cratchit mash up the potatoes and Belinda Cratchit sweeten the applesauce. And when the Christmas pudding was brought in blazing in its lighted brandy, I rejoiced along with all the Cratchits. It hardly mattered that I had never tasted a goose or a Christmas pudding and that the only food I could look forward to during the Christmas holidays was likely to be bread and herring.

When Teacher finished the story, she smiled kindly at all of us and said, "Let me now join Tiny Tim in saying, 'God Bless Us Every One' and let me also wish you all 'A Very Merry Christmas.' "

"A Very Merry Christmas to you, Miss Baxter," we all chanted, although with the exception of Lucy Palagonia and Gina Funicelli, everyone in the class was Jewish.

Miss Baxter did not open her gifts as some teachers did. She said she thought it was bad manners but she did thank us all for our thoughtfulness. Those who showed an improvement in their work and in their personal habits, she said, were giving her the finest present of all.

"My mother paid fifty cents for Teacher's gloves," Marsha Cohen boasted while we were getting our coats.

"And my mother bought a book of poems for her in a real leather binding."

"What did you give Teacher, Ruth?" Hennie Levitt asked.

I raised one eyebrow and said it was bad manners to boast. Hennie Levitt put her face up close to mine and said, "Your mother is in jail. Everybody knows your mother is in jail. I guess you're not boasting about that."

I took my coat off the hook and returned to my seat with as much dignity as I could summon.

"Jailbird!" Hennie called after me. I could hear some of the other girls in my class snickering. As much as I hated them, I hated my mother more. Teacher was looking at me, frowning. What would she think of me now?

As we filed out of our room, Miss Baxter stood by the door, wishing us all a good holiday. As I passed, she put her hand on my shoulder and gently drew me out of line. She waited until the room was empty and then she said, "I was very sorry to hear about your mother, Ruth."

I kept my eyes on the ground and began apologizing. "I'm so ashamed, Teacher . . ."

But she stopped me. "It doesn't matter in this world what others do, Ruth," she said. "Remember, you will be judged on your own merits alone."

I wanted to burst into tears, to fling myself into her arms, and tell her how humiliated I was by my mother's behavior. I wanted to tell her that she, Miss Baxter, would always be my guiding star in the future, my model of behavior, and that I would try with all my might to grow up into the kind of woman she would be proud of. But

I controlled my feelings. I looked up at her and murmured, "I'll try my best, Teacher."

She smiled and nodded approvingly at me. "Merry Christmas, Ruth," she said.

"Merry Christmas, Teacher," I answered.

My mother came home from the workhouse a week later. Two ladies came with her. Not two of her co-workers but two real ladies, one of them wrapped in a splendid fur cape and the other wearing a black satin hat with a white plume. Tanta Sadie looked around the kitchen nervously and invited them to sit down and have a glass of tea. They accepted without being asked a second or a third time. My mother yelled, "Rifka! Rifka!" as soon as she ran through the door and she picked me up off my chair and kissed me and rocked me in her arms.

"This is my daughter, my darling little girl, my Rifka," she explained to the ladies in Yiddish. My mother smelled of dirt and sweat. Her hair was unpinned and hung in greasy, unkempt locks all over her face. There was a bruise on one of her cheekbones and one of her eyes was purple. I turned away in disgust.

"Tanta Fanny," Shirley cried and she rushed forward and kissed my mother. My mother kissed and hugged her and said to the ladies, "This is my niece and my sister-in-law. This is my family."

One of the ladies, the one in the fur cape, smiled and nodded. Evidently, she couldn't understand Yiddish. The other one explained to her what my mother had said and then she smiled at me. "Little girl," she said, "you can be very proud of your mother."

"Have a glass of tea," said my aunt. "I'm sorry but I can't offer you anything else. We . . . we don't have anything in the house at the moment."

"That's all right," said the lady in the fur cape. "We've brought some refreshments along with us. After all, this is a party, isn't it?" She held out a basket that was covered with a white cloth. Inside were cakes and oranges and bread and cheese and jam and eggs.

"These ladies are from the Women's Trade Union League," my mother explained. "They have supported us ever since the strike began. I don't know what we would do without them. Today, they were waiting for me when I got out of prison. They wanted to take me home. And you know, Rifka, I rode with them on the elevated train and I didn't even get sick."

My mother ate greedily and noisily. It was disgusting, watching her. She talked and laughed and ate all at the same time, and my aunt, quietly and respectfully, kept filling everybody's glasses with tea.

"I'm so hungry," my mother cried. "I didn't eat hardly anything all the time I was there. Dry bread they gave us and burned oatmeal, and for supper, soup that smelled bad."

"Eat, eat, Fanny," urged my aunt.

"What was it like, Tanta Fanny?" Shirley asked. "Were they mean to you?"

"Not to me," said my mother, stuffing her mouth with some bread and jam. "But there was a young girl, another striker, maybe she was fifteen. And they put her in a cell with bad women, real criminals, and she cried and cried. I could hear her all night long. I wasn't exactly in a cell with high society either but I'm older and I wasn't afraid. So I said to the matron, please let her be with me . . . I said it in English like this, 'Pliss, lady, pliss let dot young girl be mit me.' See, Rifka, I said it in English. So the matron said no. She said, did I think I was on a vacation.

But later, she let the girl stay with me and then she didn't cry. They made us dress in dirty, striped dresses and we had to scrub the floors with filthy water. Ugh! I must go to the bathhouse and take a bath right away. But after a few days, the matron said she knew we weren't real criminals and she let us sew gloves and she didn't even mind if we sang songs while we worked. But it was so cold at night, and the food—like poison."

"Eat, eat," said my Tanta Sadie.

When my mother finally stopped talking, the lady in the black hat began to talk to us in Yiddish. She said public support for the strike was growing every day and that all sorts of people—teachers, social workers, students, and rich ladies—were joining the women on the picket lines. Many of the shops were beginning to give in to the strikers' demands and she thought the strike would soon be settled. She invited us to go to a big demonstration that night at Carnegie Hall.

"Carnegie Hall," I said, "where they give concerts?"

"Yes, and I think you will be very surprised when you come. Fanny, are you ready?"

"But Mrs. Bryce, I just came home."

"I know, Fanny, and I am sorry to rush you but we do have some planning to do for tonight. So get your clothes."

"But I need a bath."

"You can take one at my house."

My mother looked hungrily at me, but she went off, collected some clean clothes, and left with the two ladies.

"Don't forget—Carnegie Hall tonight!"

We ate the best supper we had eaten in weeks. Tanta Sadie said there was enough food in the basket to last a few days at least.

There were more people in Carnegie Hall that night

than there had been in Cooper Union in November. Thousands thronged the huge auditorium from the topmost gallery to the first row in the orchestra.

"Look! Look!" cried Shirley. "There's your mother."

Up on the stage, behind the speakers' platform, sat twenty girls and young women, including my mother. Each of them wore a sash with huge letters on it that proclaimed WORKHOUSE PRISONER. Above their heads hung colorful banners that said THE WORKHOUSE IS NO ANSWER TO A DEMAND FOR JUSTICE.

Farther back on the stage, about three hundred to four hundred other girls sat but their sashes only stated ARRESTED. Evidently, the twenty up in front were being honored because they had not only been arrested but had been sent to jail as well.

My mother looked clean and rosy, her hair piled neatly on top of her head, her clothes tidy. Even from where we sat, you could still see the bruises on her face. Next to her sat a small girl who seemed no bigger than myself. They talked and laughed together until the meeting began.

Speaker after speaker rose to honor the girls who had been arrested. One woman, from the Women's Trade Union League, told of the women's struggle to form a union and how perplexed they were to be told, on one hand, that they had a right to form a union and to picket and then, on the other, to be harassed by the police and punished by the courts with fines and imprisonment for exercising that right. She said they believed this country was the free harbor of all the oppressed and as good Americans, they were fighting to uphold their country's liberty.

Good Americans! My mother a good American!

After the woman finished speaking, she led forward the small girl seated next to my mother and encouraged her to tell of her experience. In a little voice, the young girl, with her hair hanging in one braid down her back and her dress only down to the top of her shoes, said that she had been taken to court as a witness because she had asked a police captain to arrest a thug who had slapped a girl. She said false witnesses had testified that she had assaulted a scab and that she was sent to the workhouse for five days without being given an opportunity to be heard.

Then each of the twenty "criminals" was introduced to the audience, and as each name was called, thousands and thousands of people cheered and applauded. When my mother was led forward, her cheeks redder than I had ever seen them, Tanta Sadie, Uncle Barney, Shirley, Morton, and Joey jumped to their feet and yelled to everybody around them, "That's Fanny! She's in our family!"

My mother began smiling, a slow smile that broadened out. She moved her head around, searching the audience while the applause continued.

"She's looking for you, Ruthie," Shirley yelled. "Stand up so she can see you."

I was confused. All around me, people were applauding for my mother, the jailbird. If she had not gone to jail, she would not be sitting on the stage of Carnegie Hall while thousands of people cheered and applauded. But Teacher had said the strikers were criminals. Teacher had said they were not good Americans. How could Teacher be mistaken?

Shirley hopped up and down in her place, shouting, "Here we are, Tanta Fanny. Here we are." She grabbed my arm and began pulling me to my feet.

My mother stuck her neck out as far as it would go. When she saw me, as Shirley pulled me to my feet, she clapped her hands together and her smile stretched all the way across the hall to where I stood.

Chapter 13

The work goes slowly.

Even though more than a year has passed since the strike ended, my mother has finished only one other napkin. She has been working on the third one since last summer and she worries.

"I don't know, I don't know," she says. "I take it with me everywhere but I'm so slow."

"Never mind, Mama," I say. "I'm only twelve years old so I won't be needing it for a while."

"I was planning to work on it this Sunday. To stay home and just work, but there's a new membership committee meeting at the union hall and they want me to sit in. But I'll only go for an hour or so, Rifka, and I'll just sit there and listen so maybe I can get a little work done."

Sit and listen? I've gone to enough meetings with my mother to know better. In the beginning, after the strike ended and my mother was invited to serve on the executive board of her union, she was still humble and awed by the union leaders. She asked me to go with her a few times in case anybody spoke in English, and she always sat quietly, her face wrinkled in painful concentration, and spoke hesitantly only when her opinion was asked.

Now she doesn't need me to go with her anymore but sometimes I go anyway. Now, she will sit in her seat and take out her embroidery and act as if she really plans on just sitting and listening. Perhaps she will begin sewing, threading her needle with some silver thread for the delicate leaves or scrolls. Perhaps she might even take a few quick stitches—until somebody begins to speak. Then the stitching will slow down. Soon the work will lie in her lap as she listens and begins to stir in her seat. If it is a large meeting, she will mutter to herself and toss around impatiently until her arm shoots up and she is on her feet, no longer shy, humble, or awed by anyone.

Except me and maybe Tanta Sadie.

"Another hat!" says my aunt. "You bought another hat and paid a dollar twenty-five for it?"

"Only a dollar twenty," says my mother sheepishly. "But Sadie, I'm going to be a delegate to the convention of the International in Boston. I can't go looking like a shlump."

My aunt remains silent. Now that my mother earns ten dollars a week and sometimes twelve when she works my aunt has little cause for grumbling—until the next strike.

"You're too busy," says my aunt. "You're always running. You're going to tire yourself out."

"But I only work fifty-four hours a week and only a

half a day on Saturday. With our new contract it will be fifty hours. I don't get tired anymore."

My mother takes great pride in her clothes—especially on the picket line. Last summer, during the big cloak-makers' strike, she bought two new organdy shirtwaists and a lightweight blue suit with silver buttons.

"It's a good thing I did," she told Tanta Sadie, "because otherwise I wouldn't have had a thing to wear to court."

She has a great respect for judges and for making a proper appearance before them.

My mother has been arrested three more times since the shirtwaist makers' strike of 1909. In each case she was not sent to prison and the union paid her fine. It doesn't bother me anymore. I suppose I'm getting used to it. But it upsets my mother. She believes firmly that every American citizen should obey the laws of this land.

"They're just arresting the wrong people," she says. "It's the bosses who cheat us out of decent wages, the crooked politicians, and the strikebreakers. They're the ones who should be arrested."

At meetings her voice can grow loud and fierce when she disagrees with her fellow union members. But in court her voice is always soft and respectful. She has developed a special cooing, coaxing voice when she speaks to policemen on the picket line.

"Good morning, Officer. How are you today?"

"You again! Lady, you sure get around."

"Well, Officer, there are some of my good friends here today and I thought I would just come and say hello."

"You better tell them not to block the sidewalks or to stop anybody from going in or . . ."

"Certainly I'll tell them and I'll also tell them they're lucky to have such a good, honest policeman protecting them from those bad strikebreakers."

"Now look, lady . . ."

"A good, working man who understands that these people aren't criminals. That they're hardworking, law-abiding citizens who only want to be paid a fair wage for a decent week's work."

"Okay, okay, you told me all that last time. I know you're going to get them singing and hollering again today like you always do and you better tell them to keep the racket down."

"Of course I will, Officer, and today we have some new songs I bet you haven't heard. Maybe I could write down the words for you."

"Lady, you sure have the gift of gab."

Everybody says she does. My mother has brought more new members into her local than anybody else.

"I don't know how she does it," says Leah Rubin. "It used to be when we went around together to visit prospective members I would do the talking and she would just listen. Now she talks and I listen. But she doesn't just talk. She laughs and she plays with the children. She drinks more tea than anybody would believe possible and she cries over every sad story she hears."

My mother sighs. "And you should hear some of the stories, Rifka. Mrs. Katz, she just joined yesterday, has three children—two of them retarded. And Hannah Levitt's father just died—but she joined anyway."

More and more now, my mother is called in to advise new locals that are springing up everywhere.

"The good times are coming," says my mother. "For

everybody, they're coming. We won our strike in 1909. The cloakmakers won theirs in 1910. People are stirring. The bosses are listening."

My mother's cheeks glow pinker and pinker as she speaks. Her dark eyes shine. People smile when they listen to her. The union is beginning to talk about making her a full-time, *paid* organizer. People I don't even know stop me on the street and say, "You're Fanny Zelitsky's daughter, aren't you? You should be proud of your mother."

Proud? I listen as my mother speaks at union meetings in rapid Yiddish, speaking so quickly sometimes her words fall into one another. In English, her speech is still broken and ungrammatical. But her voice is always passionate. Sometimes she laughs out loud, very loud, showing the space on one side of her mouth where a tooth is missing. Sometimes she cries, in front of everybody, and her fists beat at the air. She has no self-control. When she drinks tea, she drinks it from a glass, like in the old country. She holds a cube of sugar in her mouth and sips the tea through it in loud sucks. I look away. I drink my own tea now in a cup and I sip it quietly. Miss Baxter would approve.

Even though I'm now in 7B I see Miss Baxter often. I watch for her in the halls and I always say, "Good morning, Miss Baxter" or "Good afternoon, Miss Baxter." She generally returns my greeting, "Good morning, Ruth," but she never stops to talk She wears a diamond ring on her finger now and I know one day she will marry and give up teaching. I need to remember everything about her before she goes or before I graduate from grammar school next year Miss Baxter likes green. She has one shimmering green shirtwaist that she wears on special occasions and a green, fur-trimmed coat with a matching hat. Every time I pick out a new dress I pick a green one and I always try to wear a green ribbon in my hair. I study my face in the mirror. Every day it grows more and more like my mother's.

"Lucky you!" Shirley says. "You're going to be as pretty as she."

But I despair. If only I could look like Miss Baxter. I practice smiling her stiff little smile and looking at my own pink cheeks in the mirror with a frosty look in my eyes. The way she looked at me that day I asked her to return the napkin I had given her as a Christmas gift.

"Give it back?" she said.

"I know, Miss Baxter," I said, crying, the only time I ever cried before her. I knew she hated to see people cry. I knew she thought it showed a lack of self-control but I couldn't help myself.

Miss Baxter moved her chair back. We were alone in the classroom. Everybody else had gone home. It was the day after the big meeting in Carnegie Hall.

"I know," I continued, sobbing, "it's very bad manners to ask for a gift back and I'm sorry but there was no money and I wanted to give you something special."

"I told the class over and over again," said Miss Baxter, impatiently, "that I didn't want any gifts."

"It was wrong, Teacher, but I wanted you to know how much you meant to me," I hiccuped through my sobs, feeling her frosty eyes on my face. I had worked so hard to gain her good opinion and now was I to lose it? After this would she let me hold the flag again? Would she pick somebody else to water the plants? Huge tears dripped off my chin.

"Control yourself, Ruth," said Miss Baxter. "Don't

you have a handkerchief? There's no reason to carry on like this. I haven't used the napkin yet and I will return it to you tomorrow."

I looked at her hopefully. Perhaps she would forgive me if I explained about my mother. "My mother made the napkin for my trousseau. There was a tablecloth and five other napkins too, but somebody stole it on the boat coming over. She cried for days. I think she would die if she knew I gave it away."

"Now, Ruth . . ."

"She would, she would, Teacher! Because she made it in the old country when we . . . when there were just the two of us. It means a lot to her because she never pawned it even when she pawned everything else. But maybe she can make you something else, Miss Baxter. Maybe I'll ask her to make you a different napkin."

"I don't want anything from your mother, Ruth. Let's just forget the whole thing."

Of course. Miss Baxter did not want anything from my mother because she did not consider her a good American. Perhaps if I could show her that she had been mistaken.

"My mother was on the stage at Carnegie Hall, Miss Baxter. There were thousands of people—some of them were rich—some of them were teachers—and they clapped for her."

I saw myself inside Miss Baxter's eyes. Inside her pupils, two little me's were reflected, two little immigrant girls. In her eyes that's all I could ever be.

Her stiff fingers touched my shoulders quickly. "It's all over now, Ruth, so just pull yourself together. I will return your napkin tomorrow."

She rose from her chair and guided me to the door.

"Teacher," I began.

"Good afternoon, Ruth," she said.

My mother doesn't smell of perfume and her hands are not smooth and white like Miss Baxter's. Sometimes she sops up the gravy on her plate with pieces of bread. I tell her in America it is not considered good manners. She looks embarrassed when I tell her and promises not to do it again but she forgets.

Often now, my mother and I are embarrassed with each other. She tries to talk to me about her union activities and sometimes I go to meetings with her. I try to talk to her about school and my new friends. I read her some of my compositions and repeat what Miss Fuller, my present teacher, says about my work. I tell her about Laura Birnbaum and Nettie Cooper, my two friends. I don't need Shirley anymore now that I have my own friends. When we get into bed at night both of us fall right to sleep. We don't argue anymore. She goes her way and I go mine.

My friends never call me stuck-up. Maybe because they are even more stuck-up than I. Laura wants to be a dentist and Nettie reads all the time. We belong to a book discussion group at the Educational Alliance and sometimes on Sundays we go to museums and concerts.

I try to tell my mother and she tries to listen. She doesn't always understand and sometimes she asks strange, awkward questions. She never stops talking about her union and sometimes I get bored. Often, she has an eye on the clock and jumps up while I am talking to her to run off to a meeting or some other activity. She is embarrassed, apologetic, and I am embarrassed too. We always say how we should spend more time together. Now that she no longer gets sick on the Third Avenue El, she keeps saying we should go uptown one Sunday and walk in Central Park. I wonder if we ever will. She never has the time.

So I'm glad I got the napkin back. Because she made it for me when we had all the time. Back in the old country when the two of us loved each other better than anybody else in the whole world. I had nearly forgotten all about it but when my mother smiled at me that night in Carnegie Hall, I remembered. Across that big room, it was only me that she smiled at.

I thought I was getting the napkin back for her but now I think it was for me. Because I had nearly forgotten what it was like back there. Bubba and Zader are both dead now and I can't even remember what Bubba's poppy seed cookies tasted like. The second napkin that my mother made is very beautiful, maybe more beautiful even than the first. But I can tell the difference. And when I hold it in my hand I can almost remember how my mother used to make garlands for my hair.

I wonder if she ever will finish the twelve napkins and the tablecloth. I hope she will because I like to daydream about the future. I like to see myself in the years to come when I am a teacher like Miss Baxter, dressed in a beautiful green silk dress, giving a Thanksgiving dinner for my own family. Of course my mother will be there, Tanta Sadie, Uncle Barney, Shirley, and the boys. Maybe I will have a husband and children. They are dim in my mind but my Thanksgiving table is not dim. It glows with fine crystal and expensive china. And best and most beautiful of all are the splendid white embroidered tablecloth and napkins that my mother made for my trousseau.

"I'll be back no later than three or four," says my mother.

"Don't worry, Mama, I'll probably be out with my friends."

"That's all right, Rifka," she says. "You go and have a good time. I'll come home and work on the napkin by myself."

"There's lots of time," I tell her. "I'm not getting married in a hurry. And who knows? Maybe I'll never get married."

"Bite your tongue," says my mother, shocked. "Of course you'll get married."

"Well, you're not exactly hurrying to get married, Fanny," says my aunt.

We all know who she is thinking of. She is thinking of Mr. Rosenberg, who comes over to visit my mother from time to time. We all like him very much—all of us except my mother.

She draws herself up and says proudly, "I . . . I should marry a boss! A man who doesn't even run a union shop! Besides, Rifka, it's different for me. I was married. I had a child. I had you."

Proud? Am I proud of my mother with her loud voice, her coarse hands, and her poor table manners?

We look at each other across the room. It has been a long, long time since she made that first napkin and we played together in the fields. Does it seem that long ago and that far away to her too? Maybe one day I'll tell her how I gave away the napkin and asked for it back. I wonder if she knows how precious it is to me.

We turn away from each other in embarrassment. She folds the napkin and puts it into her bag.

"I won't be long, Rifka," she murmurs.

"Call me Ruth," I tell her.

Afterword

There really was a Shirtwaist Makers' Strike in 1909 in which twenty thousand young girls and women, mostly immigrants, conducted a successful strike in New York's garment district. Without trained leaders, they managed to maintain orderly picket lines, face arrest and imprisonment, and resist police provocation and physical assaults by hired strikebreakers. Their courage, determination, and good nature captured the imagination of the public. Others joined their picket lines—suffragettes, socially prominent women and reformers who, like Ida Tarbell, understood that their struggle was "not merely for themselves but for society as a whole. Anything which improves their condition must improve everything in the town . . . the struggle for one is the struggle for all."

134

All of the details of the strike are taken from contemporary sources. I would like to express my appreciation to the International Ladies' Garment Workers' Union for allowing me to do research in its archives.